The Journey Prize Anthology

Winners of the $10,000 Journey Prize

1989
Holley Rubinsky for "Rapid Transits"

1990
Cynthia Flood for "My Father Took a Cake to France"

1991
Yann Martel for "The Facts Behind the Helsinki Roccamatios"

1992
Rozena Maart for "No Rosa, No District Six"

1993
Gayla Reid for "Sister Doyle's Men"

1994
Melissa Hardy for "Long Man the River"

1995
Kathryn Woodward for "Of Marranos and Gilded Angels"

1996
Elyse Gasco for "Can You Wave Bye Bye, Baby?"

1997 (shared)
Gabriella Goliger for "Maladies of the Inner Ear"
Anne Simpson for "Dreaming Snow"

1998
John Brooke for "The Finer Points of Apples"

1999
Alissa York for "The Back of the Bear's Mouth"

2000
Timothy Taylor for "Doves of Townsend"

2001
Kevin Armstrong for "The Cane Field"

The Journey Prize Anthology

Short Fiction from the Best of
Canada's New Writers

Selected by André Alexis, Derek McCormack,
and Diane Schoemperlen

M&S

National Library of Canada Cataloguing in Publication

National Library of Canada has catalogued this publication as follows:

The Journey Prize anthology : the best short fiction from Canada's literary journals.

Subtitle varies.
Annual.
1-
ISSN 1197-0693
ISBN 0-7710-4419-4 (vol. 14)

1. Short stories, Canadian (English) 2. Canadian fiction (English) – 20th century.

PS8329.J68   C813'.0108054   C93-039053-9
PR9197.32.J68

We acknowledge the financial support of the Government of Canada through the Book Publishing Industry Development Program for our publishing activities. We further acknowledge the support of the Canada Council for the Arts and the Ontario Arts Council for our publishing program.

"Cogagwee" © Mike Barnes; "Listen" © Geoffrey Brown; "Miss Canada" © Jocelyn Brown; "What Remains" © Emma Donoghue; "You Are a Spaceman With Your Head Under the Bathroom Stall Door" © Jonathan Goldstein; "Confidence Men" © Robert McGill; "The Stars Are Falling" © Robert McGill; "Philemon" © Nick Melling; "Alex the God" © Robert Mullen; "The Pool" © Karen Munro; "Being Famous" © Leah Postman; "Green Fluorescent Protein" © Neil Smith.
These stories are reprinted with permission of the authors.

Typeset in Trump Mediaeval by M&S, Toronto
Printed and bound in Canada

McClelland & Stewart Ltd.
The Canadian Publishers
481 University Avenue
Toronto, Ontario
M5G 2E9
www.mcclelland.com

1 2 3 4 5   06 05 04 03 02

About the Journey Prize Anthology

The $10,000 Journey Prize is awarded annually to a new and developing writer of distinction. This award, now in its fourteenth year, and given for the second time in association with the Writers' Trust of Canada as the Writers' Trust of Canada/ McClelland & Stewart Journey Prize, is made possible by James A. Michener's generous donation of his Canadian royalty earnings from his novel *Journey*, published by McClelland & Stewart in 1988. The winner of this year's Journey Prize will be selected from among the twelve stories in this book.

The Journey Prize Anthology comprises a selection from submissions made by literary journals across Canada, and, in recognition of the vital role journals play in discovering new writers, McClelland & Stewart makes its own award of $2,000 to the journal that has submitted the winning entry. This year the selection jury comprises three acclaimed authors: André Alexis is the author of *Despair & Other Stories of Ottawa* and *Childhood*, which won the Chapters/Books in Canada First Novel Award, shared the Trillium Award, and was shortlisted for The Giller Prize and the Rogers Communications Writers' Trust Fiction Prize. He lives in Toronto, where he is at work on a new novel, *Asylum*. Derek McCormack is the author of the short story collections *Dark Rides* and *Wish Book*. He is also the co-author of *Wild Mouse*, which was nominated for the City of Toronto Book Award. He lives in Toronto, where he works at an independent bookstore. Diane Schoemperlen is the author of the novels *In the Language of Love*, a finalist for the Smithbooks/Books in Canada First Novel Award, and *Our Lady of the Lost and Found*, and six books of short fiction, including *Forms of Devotion*, winner of the Governor General's Award, and, most recently, *Red Plaid Shirt: Stories New and Selected*. She lives in Kingston.

The Journey Prize Anthology has established itself as one of the most prestigious anthologies in the country. It has become a who's who of up-and-coming writers, and many of the authors whose early work has appeared in the anthology's pages have gone on to single themselves out with collections of short stories and literary awards. The Journey Prize itself is the most significant monetary award given in Canada to a writer at the beginning of his or her career for a short story or excerpt from a fiction work in progress.

McClelland & Stewart would like to acknowledge the continuing enthusiastic support of writers, literary journal editors, and the public in the common celebration of the emergence of new voices in Canadian fiction.

For more information about the *Journey Prize Anthology*, please consult our Web site: www.mcclelland.com/jpa

Contents

INTRODUCTION

It was an interesting year.

Yes, "interesting" is one of the words one least wants to hear in response to one's work, but sometimes no other word will do.

The Canadian short story is changing.

The old way of doing stories still has its practitioners, but Alice Munro and Mavis Gallant, for instance, no longer provide the chief models from which stories are written.

Not this year, anyway, not if the stories we read are representative.

Which is not to suggest any other model had precedence, either. We were just as likely to read stories influenced by Gertrude Stein, Michael Ondaatje, Diane Schoemperlen . . . (stories that were magic realist, postmodernist, minimalist . . .) as those influenced by the old (and still lovely) Chekhovian/Munrovian ideals.

We read eighty-two stories, each selected by the editors of literary journals as representing the "best" of the stories they published in 2001. Quite a cull, then, and quite a task. They have our gratitude. (In fact, it would be more accurate to say that the stories we received are representative of what journal editors feel is the best work being done in Canada.)

The three of us (Derek McCormack, Diane Schoemperlen, André Alexis) are writers with different sensibilities, so we (tacitly) accepted that this year's anthology should reflect something of the range of our individual aesthetics, the range of fictional strategies available to Canadian writers.

The point of our selection was not to give place to aesthetics, however.

We were chiefly interested in work that moved us: aesthetically, emotionally, intellectually.

The striking narrative voice of Jocelyn Brown's "Miss Canada" . . .

The humour of "Green Fluorescent Protein" . . .

The trance-inducing rhythm of "Listen" . . .

These stories made sense, irrespective of their origins, and they held us.

It is gratifying to have such pleasing encounters with new work and, of course, encounter is the essential pleasure.

There are other pleasures, though.

For instance, it was a relief to discover the humour and play at work in the best of this year's stories. Yes, many of the stories we read were self-consciously serious, civic-minded and plodding, but the ones we admired were, for the most part, wonderfully amusing. They are ironic ("What Remains"), bitter ("Being Famous"), absurd ("The Pool"), mysterious ("The Stars Are Falling"), filled with one-liners ("You Are a Spaceman With Your Head Under the Bathroom Stall Door"), but humorous. They come at you from an unexpected angle.

In a time in which no single way of writing has clear hegemony, it is perhaps to be expected that humour (or its sister, distance) assumes greater importance. This year, few writers were certain about certainty.

It was also fascinating to discover how different writers dealt with similar concerns. The past is dealt with mockingly ("Alex the God"), gently ("What Remains"), or like a jigsaw puzzle ("Cogagwee"), but the three writers (Mullen, Donoghue, and Barnes) strive to coax a notion of the "heroic" into the present.

Similarly, the stories that play with popular culture ("Being Famous," "Green Fluorescent Protein," "Miss Canada," "You Are a Spaceman . . .") do so in various ways, while striving to make place for the day-to-day, to make room for other versions of the heroic.

And again: in a year in which the certain is uncertain, the most honest work is almost always an effort to salvage something of worth: a voice, a moment, a coming to awareness, a past . . .

If this sounds as if we were looking for stories that satisfied our curiosity about pop culture or history . . . this introduction has given the wrong impression. The work we've selected is inevitably about more (and less) than can be said in an introduction. (What is there to say about "Listen" or "Miss Canada" save that you should, maybe, find your own meanings in them, if meaning is something you want in a story?)

The similarities are discovered after the fact.

The stories we've chosen are the raw material from which versions of our country (its sensibilities, its possibilities . . .) and our time (its morals, its culture . . .) might be reconstructed.

We would like to thank McClelland & Stewart for their support of new writers, and the editors and publishers of the journals and magazines whose efforts make the publication of this annual anthology possible.

It was an interesting year.

André Alexis
Derek McCormack
Diane Schoemperlen
Toronto, August 2002

ROBERT MULLEN

Alex the God

Isn't it always the first sign of a god that he astounds? Certainly nothing in the world could have been more astounding than the news reaching the suq that day from Issus that mighty Darius, the King of Kings, had been defeated, that his Persian army had been routed by an upstart Greek, by a Macedonian no less, by a mere boy of a king whose name we were hearing for the very first time.

"Now we're in for it," I told my wife. "They say he's headed south."

"In for what, my heart? In for war? Should we start hoarding food?"

My mind raced ahead. My wife was the rock, the practical one, whereas I – I liked to think – possessed the vision. Why should there necessarily be war? What, after all, was Darius to us? We were business people here, not soldiers, and business was war enough.

"We can hide the children," my wife said. "We can board up the shop."

"I'll deal with the children," I said. "You can make a sign."

"A sign, balm of my eyes? But what should it say?"

"*Greek Spoken Here.*"

The children had been playing in the hills, but now that would have to stop. Our two children, little Rosie and Yusuf Junior, when I picked them up, smelled delightfully of wild thyme.

"Listen. Try to remember. What have I told you about opportunity?"

Their small faces remained blank. So often, when dealing with children, one felt one was wasting one's breath.

"The man who waits for opportunity to knock . . . ," my wife prompted.

"Is already too late!" little Rosie screamed with joy.

Dear little Rosie! I kissed the top of her head. I kissed my son Yusuf as well. This was a moment for which I must have been waiting for some time, perhaps even for all of my life, for now that that moment had finally arrived I knew exactly what I would do. Under Darius we had been content – content but not ecstatic.

"Isn't it dangerous?" My wife clutched the sleeve of my robe. "What if you don't come back? What business is it of ours who rules the world?"

Exactly. What did it matter who ruled the world, so long as someone did? If not Darius, then Alexander, and if Alexander – and this was what I meant by vision – then why not be the first to welcome him?

I had guessed just where I would find him. The army was at ease, lounging on the banks of the Dog River while, on the cliffs above, Alexander and his generals were busy carving their names into the limestone where every tyrant who had ever passed this way had carved his name before them. And yet here at last was something new, here was a king scarcely out of his teens, a king with golden curls.

"Well, well," I said. "Just through the door and already writing on the walls."

My makeshift Greek was obviously understood. I was seized, roughly, and my arms were twisted behind my back.

"What was that, greaseball? A fart? No one speaks that way to a king!"

This was just what I was counting on. The king turned to look, regarding me at first with utter disbelief; then, just as I had hoped, his curiosity got the better of him.

"That will do, Heff. Breaking arms won't win us any friends."

My arms were freed. Cautiously, using just two fingers, I reached into the sleeve of my robe and pulled out a card:

Yusuf Maruf
Fine Carpets
Sidon, Phoenicia

"You see, Heff? That's all it is. He wants to sell us some rugs."

"Carpets, effendi. From all over the world. At prices everyone can afford."

Alexander, the king of the Greeks, giggled at this like a schoolgirl.

"Good prices, did you say? Tell him, Heff, what we paid for Darius's carpets."

This got a good laugh. So be it. Greek humour wasn't Phoenician humour. I waited for Alexander to compose himself.

"But who are you really, Yusuf? That's the question. That's to say, how can I use you, when I have so many men already?"

"So many soldiers, effendi."

Alexander's face darkened. His eyes bored into me, his strangely mismatched eyes, one being blue, just as you would have expected, but the other for some reason being brown.

"Get him a blanket, Heff. Tell him the password. He might just be right."

The halt was over. Suddenly the landscape came alive again. Soldiers who a moment before had been lounging on the river-bank, filling goatskins and washing their socks, were now everywhere scrambling for their weapons and their helmets, and forming themselves into a line of march. As for me, as soon as Alexander's attention turned elsewhere I found myself once more in an armlock.

"Why wait, greaser? Why drag this out? Why not confess?"

"My name's Yusuf," I said coolly. "Can't you pronounce it?"

"I wouldn't put myself to the trouble. I know the type. Either you're an assassin or you're a little stinker of a spy – and just wait until I find out which!"

Two things I would never forget about that day, the dust through which we marched and the angry glare of the man riding beside me on horseback. Heff was Hephaestion, Alexander's lifelong companion and bodyguard, ordinarily Alexander's shadow but at that moment mine.

At dusk that great army, having received the order, simply stopped in its tracks and sat down. Fires were lit. I was thrown a filthy blanket. The password for that night was "Rhinoceros." I could smell bread and roast meat. I ate a few dates from my pocket. Then, as I was dozing off, I found myself yanked to my feet.

"Up! He wants you, greaser. Just keep your hands where I can see them."

Alexander's tent showed slivers of light; within, the king bent over a map.

"Have a look, Yusuf. Here's where we are and here's Sidon. It seems to have got itself right in our way."

"Please don't say that, effendi. Why fight if you don't have to?"

I laid it out for him. Darius having been defeated but not overthrown, there were bound to be some, men of little vision or imagination, who would continue to prefer the devil that they knew and attempt to raise the populace in defense of the past. The way to overcome them without bloodshed was simply to make Sidon a better offer, a view of a better future.

"And how would I go about that, my friend?"

"Sidon prefers business to war, effendi. Come as our guest, as a customer. Shop. Visit the suq . . ."

"And then slip into the city?"

"And then slip into our hearts, effendi."

Alexander decided at once. He straightened. He brushed aside the stones holding down the map, which curled up of its own accord. Alexander stood, I couldn't help noticing, like someone who wished he were taller.

"What time is it? Damn this darkness anyway. Let's have some music, Heff."

A musician was summoned. The man appeared still in his night attire. Placing himself upon a stool, he unpacked his lute and commenced the delicate business of tuning the strings.

"Enough of that," Alexander barked. "Get on with it. Compensate."

With the very first notes, Alexander's shoulders began to relax. His head lolled to one side, to the left. His foot began keeping time with what he seemed to take to be the beat.

"I played myself once. Didn't I, Heff? Until I was told that it wasn't manly."

This was difficult to believe. How could anyone with any appreciation of music bear to hear it played on an instrument which was only half-tuned? What could he be thinking? What else did he hear when he seemed to be hearing music? By the time the king at last began to yawn, it was nearly dawn.

"Excellent," Alexander then congratulated the musician. "Each and every note in its place. Just like my army. Pay the man, Heff."

What would at once have been obvious to any spy was that it was not the size of Alexander's army which was to be feared, but its discipline. At dawn, with scarcely a sound other than the scuffing of feet, the army reformed for the march south. To the fore the infantry took its position, the famous phalanx, and aligned behind was the cavalry, horses and men alike as still as statues, and to this body were attached two wings of Cretan archers, their sharpshooters' eyes already squeezed half-shut.

A cheer went up as the king now appeared, mounted on his favourite horse, Bucephalas. Armour creaked; livery squealed. From the start everyone was in step. An army of tens of thousands set off as one man beneath the yellow sun, beside the sparkling blue sea, and that one man, of course, was Alexander.

Hephaestion this time placed me with the mercenaries, that curious ragbag contingent of sunworshippers, hook-nosed nomads, red-haired Thracians, and ferocious Ethiopians, these last dressed in the skins of wild animals.

"Try to keep up, greaser, that's my advice. Stragglers are cut off at the waist."

We baked in the sun. We breathed in dust. At midday, when everyone else was resting, I was once again summoned to Alexander, who this time was holding a letter.

"Well? Do you see who it's from? You know, I suppose, who Aristotle is."

"Doesn't he write books, effendi?"

"Yes he does, and I've taken him to task over that. Should wisdom be for sale in market stalls?"

Without waiting for my answer, he picked up a second letter – and I caught a whiff of perfume. As he read his lips moved, mumbling the words out loud.

"*From Olympias the queen to her dear darling boy Alex, greetings.*"

I began to fidget. The letter, surely, was meant to be personal. No doubt Greek ideas were different but there was too much talk here, for my liking, of kisses and caresses. Beyond this string of endearments, however, the mood of the letter suddenly changed and Alexander's with it. Why, if he loved her, Olympias asked, had Alexander, after Issus, allowed Darius to escape?

Suddenly every muscle in Alexander's body tensed.

"What could I do? What does she expect? Battles end in confusion and smoke."

"Mothers are mothers, effendi. Some even more so than others."

Alexander read on. Olympias advised him to take Sidon by storm. Sidon, reduced to ashes, would be a warning to all the other cities in his path. Now I really did have reason to squirm.

"Maybe I should go, effendi. These are military matters."

"Take care, my friend. You can go when I dismiss you. I may be a king, but I have feelings."

"I would never have doubted that, effendi."

"Then show some consideration. There's a human being beneath this armour, and a human being deserves respect. Never, ever, if you want to live to sell another carpet, walk away while I'm talking to myself."

Sidon, as every schoolchild now knows, fell without a fight. Quick on its feet, Sidon, by and large, saw sense. Those too slow in shifting their allegiances were apprehended, shaved bald, bound with anchor chains, and presented to Alexander with the city's compliments.

"Why not finish the job?" Hephaestion raged. "Hair can always grow back."

But Alexander kept his word. No blood was shed. Misplaced, untimely loyalty was still loyalty Alexander dismounted, removed his helmet, shook out his golden curls, and we set off into the suq.

"You're welcome, effendi. You're more than welcome. We'll put up a plaque."

The truth was, I feared for his life. In the dim light of the suq a determined enemy, one hothead with a knife, could have changed history. But only children confronted us, harmless urchins, bug-eyed, mouths ajar, muttering: *Iskandar! Iskandar!*

There was barely room in the shop for three. Our shop was small and cluttered, carpets being stacked from the floor to the ceiling. While Alexander browsed, Hephaestion remained in the doorway with his hand on the grip of his sword.

"Look at the colours first, effendi. The dyes should all be natural."

"The colours I'll leave to you, my friend. Just tell me what they're about."

What was there to tell? What was any carpet about? What wasn't it about? Why open that can of worms?

"Look closely, effendi. What you can see, what you can feel, is what it's about."

"Go carefully, my friend. Remember who you're dealing with. All I can see are crooked lines."

"In that case turn the carpet over, effendi. Examine the workmanship."

"No need. You'd hardly tell me that if I was likely to spot any faults."

Alexander was out of his depth and the kindest thing was to put him out of his misery. I suggested that I might use my own experience to select those carpets which would be worthy of him.

"You do that, Yusuf. I'll leave you to it. I only want what's best for me."

With that he would have been out the door had Hephaestion not been blocking it.

"Just a minute. Not so fast. How will we know that we're getting his best price?"

"You'll know," I said, refusing to be bullied in my own shop, "because there's only one price. Only the fair price."

"You must think that we're chumps then . . ."

"Pay him what he asks, Heff." Alexander was a king, not a quibbler. "Either that, or confiscate them. A man needs to be able to look himself in the eye."

By the time they had gone, I was shaking. I could have done with changing my clothes. My wife, who had heard everything from behind a curtain, now appeared to greet me, to cover my hands with kisses.

"Balm of my heart!" she said in all sincerity.

"It's over now," I told her. "Anything might have happened, but it didn't."

"Feast of my eyes! O daylight returning!"

We chose the carpets together. Even if Alexander was no judge, I wanted him to have the best. Every one of our carpets, I liked to tell customers, was a magic carpet; simply looking closely at a carpet could transport you, could carry you off to a distant land.

"Will he pay, do you think?" my wife asked.

"Even if he doesn't," I said, "this will always be where he shopped."

I went by myself with the bundle of carpets. The army was settled for the night, spread out under our olive trees. Some of the men held tiny nightingales on skewers over their fires. The password for that evening was "Hottentot," every repetition of which, Alexander had no doubt calculated, would further whet the men's appetite for adventure.

I found him alone, pacing the floor of his tent and soaked with sweat. He looked terrible; he looked terrified.

"It's the usual thing," he said. "I must have dozed off. I had that dream again."

"What dream, effendi? A nightmare? Everyone has bad dreams."

"Like mine? I doubt that, my friend. I seriously doubt that."

There was a pitcher of wine on the table. I started to pour some into a goblet for him, but he snatched the pitcher and tipped it up, quaffing the wine like water, which left him with a purple moustache.

"She's in bed, Yusuf. The queen is. Olympias. The thing is, she's naked."

"Your own mother, effendi?"

"The same, my friend. And then the snake appears. Olympias, excited, throws open her arms . . ."

"Please, effendi. That's enough. Here we respect mothers."

"Well that's certainly your prerogative, my friend."

He tipped up the pitcher again. The wine this time dribbled down his chin. It appeared to revive him. His eyes flashed mischievously. The race of men was divided, he started saying then, into those who were mad and those who were fools.

"Fools, at least, can sleep peacefully. They could, that is, except for men like me."

"Like you, effendi? But madmen, surely, don't win battles."

"Don't they? How can you be sure? Wait until you've seen a battle."

Where was Hephaestion? I had promised my wife I wouldn't be long. The king now filled a goblet to the brim and thrust this upon me.

"Battles are chaos, Yusuf. That's my whole point. What does a sane man know about chaos?"

"No more than he's forced to know, effendi."

"Exactly. He goes through life without ever knowing life. But here's the thing, my friend. I could use someone around me who's sane."

"But I'm a married man, effendi, with two children to raise."

"Yes I know. Life clearly agrees with you. But does someone like me come along every day?"

His eyes sparkled. My legs were suddenly like jelly.

"You expect me to drop everything? To leave people in the lurch?"

"You speak the language, my friend. You know the lay of the land. Sort things out first, by all means, but be ready to march by dawn."

"By dawn, effendi? That's impossible. You don't realize what's involved."

"Perhaps not, but that's *my* prerogative. I see only what I need to see. In the face of chaos, that at least gives me a ghost of a chance."

(II)

Next in Alexander's way was Tyre, and Tyre had ideas of its own. Tyre, we found, had dug in its heels and was preparing for a fight. Tyre, defiant on its island, its proud profile still a spotless white against the blue of sky and sea, was daring Alexander to do his worst.

"So it's war then. Bloody war. Prepare the men, Heff. Perhaps it's time we got back to doing things the hard way."

"Now he's talking, greaser. What's Tyre to us? Take one last look."

For days the orders flew thick and fast, often in Greek too rapid for me to follow, but the results were clear enough. Before Tyre could be attacked a siege mole had to be built, a causeway to the island from the shore. And when the first mole failed, swept away one night by a storm, a second mole was begun at once, this time shored up with boulders and trees, fruit trees, orange and olive trees which for good measure were winched out by their roots.

Only Hephaestion could see the bright side of such wanton destruction.

"The fewer the trees, greaser, the fewer the spies."

Hephaestion, too, was blonde. Hephaestion, whose hair was dyed and curled, bore a superficial resemblance to Alexander, enough to give an assassin pause, to create confusion in the would-be assassin's mind, Hephaestion hoped, and so put off his aim.

Alexander himself was everywhere. Just as Aristotle, the teacher, had divided the day between metaphysics and rhetoric, so Alexander, the pupil, first held council with his officers and then mingled with the men, discussing strategy in the mornings and tactics in the afternoons.

In his tent one evening we discussed theology. Priests were behind the trouble in Tyre, Alexander's spies had reported.

Priests from the temple of Melqart were using every priestly trick they knew to keep up the people's spirits.

"And who's Melqart?" Alexander demanded. "Why wasn't I told?"

Who was Melqart? Who was any god? What was known as Adonis on one bank of the river was known as something else entirely on the other side. What was called Ashmun in Sidon was called Melqart in Tyre. Religion, to a businessman, meant having a good memory for names.

"It's been said, effendi, that the black man's god is black. A dog's god barks."

"Go on. And what's behind it all? What is it that barks?"

Yes what? What could it be that barked? An essence? A form? A paradigm? Dogness? Or was the bark all in the mind of the beholder?

"Perhaps, effendi, a god is simply man's highest aspiration."

"Perhaps, Yusuf. I admire your optimism, but I'm hardly convinced."

In that case, why speculate? Why swim out of our depth? Why not wait a little, I suggested to Alexander, and then Melqart himself would be in our hands.

"To know about a god, effendi, why not ask a god?"

"A defeated god? A discredited god? A shell of a god? Surely, my friend, men of intelligence can do better than that."

Tyre was doomed. The second mole stayed solid, withstanding not only storms but also the sappers who swam out each night from the city to try to undermine it. Melqart had had his day, and Tyre's makeshift windmills for deflecting arrows were no match for powerful catapults.

Alexander, as we watched, asked what news I had had from my wife.

"The usual thing, effendi. Business could be better. The children are out of control."

"Nothing about siege moles then? Nothing about doing a job right the first time?"

"Nothing, effendi. She's not political. And you, any word from Olympias?"

"Take a guess, my friend. Take a fucking guess."

Alexander led the final assault, which was a mere formality. Tyre's fate had long since been sealed. The day after there were games, with captured soldiers made to race against one another in full armor under a blazing sun. Old men competed in sack races for their lives, Jews rolled hoops, and in the evening the women of the city who had survived were forced to dance for us.

This was pathetic. Reduced to skin and bones the women barely had the strength to shuffle their feet. Why put them through this? For whose benefit? Alexander, I noticed, was tapping his foot. Wearying at last of the sad spectacle, he whispered something to Hephaestion, who came and passed the order to me.

"Tell them that's enough, greaser. Except for that one on the end. He wants to see her in his tent tonight."

What was I to do? The woman stared at me with huge hollow eyes. She was bereaved, she was starving. I explained in our own language what was expected of her, adding off my own bat that what had attracted Alexander was her dignity under these difficult circumstances.

The woman's mouth fell open; she was missing several teeth.

"Why are you doing this?" she asked. "You're not even a Greek."

"No, I'm not. A Greek would have dragged you by the hair."

We stopped outside the tent. The air was bitter with smoke. It would be a long time before Tyre was Tyre again.

"I'm sorry. You'll have to undress first. They don't trust anyone an inch."

As the woman slipped in, Hephaestion stomped out.

"Something wrong, greaser? Crows got your tongue? She wasn't too skinny to throw stones, was she?"

I waited there, holding the woman's clothes. Tyre was ruined, burned, with scarcely a building left standing, but no doubt there were still cellars, sheds, cisterns, boltholes, and the least I could do for her, once her ordeal was over, was see her safely to some home.

Olympias must have been furious. Too much time had been wasted at Tyre, too much had been left to chance. Gaza was the next stop, and for Gaza Olympias had come up with a plan. Hephaestion and I were to ride ahead, ahead even of the vanguard, posing as merchants in order to buy up grain.

"That's dirty," Hephaestion protested. "That's underhanded. Why not beat them fair and square?"

"Just do it," Alexander ordered. "Take mules. No armour and no rough stuff."

All around us lay desolation. There were no orchards left, no stones, no birds and no hares; every spring had been sucked dry, every well exhausted, and the road to either side of us was lined with the crosses of crucified priests.

"You'd better leave the talking to me," I warned Hephaestion.

"When it comes to kissing asses, greaser, be my guest."

A plan was no better than its execution. Hephaestion, on a donkey, was unlikely to fool anyone. His feet, as he rode, dragged two furrows in the ground.

"Sit further back. It's not a horse. Let your legs stick out to the sides."

Hephaestion's legs flapped furiously. He was a soldier and he had always been a soldier. In his whole life he had never wanted to be anything but a soldier and even as a boy, Hephaestion recalled as we rode, he had taken his orders only from Alexander.

"He didn't mess about, greaser. We didn't walk to school, we marched."

The day was hot. Hephaestion's grey tunic was stained with sweat. At the end of each day, even as a schoolboy, Alexander had written a report on his day's activities for his mother, who later sent him back her corrections.

"That's how these things start, greaser. Back then it was cute."

"And Philip?" I said. "King Philip?"

"Absent without leave. Out screwing whatever moved."

Slowly the land around us was returning to life. The first birds reappeared. We came to an orange grove; the trees were in full bloom, and beneath them men in small groups were standing talking. Hephaestion, forgetting for the moment Alexander's orders, pulled up his donkey and, out of habit, reached for where his sword should have been.

"This stinks, greaser. What's it all about?"

"Nothing," I said. "They're just enjoying themselves."

"At this time of day?"

Who would be Hephaestion? Who would be a Greek? Who wanted the whole world for an enemy? I almost felt sorry for him.

"Wave," I said. "A merchant has to get along with everyone."

"Then we're fucked, that's what."

"Not necessarily. Just don't make a fist when you wave."

Barley and wheat grew on terraces, terrace upon terrace rising up from the sea, and we would have to visit each one of them, convincing the suspicious farmers that we were here as merchants, as businessmen, in all innocence, motivated solely by greed.

"Stop gritting your teeth," I told Hephaestion. "Smile. Be friendly. And don't worry. No one's going to believe for a moment that you really mean it."

So, thanks to Olympias's prescience, what had dragged on for seven months at Tyre took only two at Gaza. Gaza, already weakened by a shortage of grain, was no match for the boulders hurled by Alexander's giant slingshots. What Olympias couldn't have foreseen, however, was that Gaza, before succumbing, would get off a lucky shot.

Hearing that Alexander had taken an arrow hit, I confronted Hephaestion.

"How did it happen? Weren't you with him? Whose body were you guarding anyway, your own?"

"Shut up, greaser. This is for men. This is for those who know what wounds are."

The wound was to his shoulder. By the time I reached Alexander's tent, his arm was already in a sling. With shaking hands I poured myself a cup of wine.

"Calm down, my friend. Don't be such an old woman. How many of those do I need in my life?"

"But why do it, effendi? Why expose yourself? Why take such risks?"

"Exactly what someone else will be wanting to know. Bring me my writing box."

This was the chest in which he kept his correspondence. Amidst the hundreds of letters from Olympias there was also a small neat packet containing those sent by Aristotle. Reason, apparently, was concise, while love was voluminous.

I spread some blank parchment and offered him his quill pen.

"No, Yusuf, you do it. Tell her I was out hunting."

He was feverish. After scribbling the note to Olympias, I made him a hot drink with herbs. About this time Hephaestion came in, took one look at Alexander shivering on the couch, and turned on his heels.

"Who was that, Yusuf? Was it Philip? Did he say what he wanted?"

"Your father, effendi? But your father's dead."

"Yes he is, but who killed him? Tell me that while we're on the subject."

All I knew was what I had heard, that one of Philip's own catamites had murdered him during a fit of jealousy. Alexander laughed at this. Did he know something different, or was he merely delirious?

"Look at me, Yusuf. Closely. Who do I take after?"

"Well, you must take after your father, effendi."

"Exactly. So isn't it strange that I bear no resemblance to Philip?"

This was not the sort of talk I liked. Why was Alexander so intent on befouling his mother, whom he obviously loved? I tried to cover him with a blanket, but he threw it off.

"He knew it, my friend, I can assure you. The very sight of me infuriated him."

"You're burning up, effendi. You're confused. One can always find a resemblance if one looks hard enough."

"No, my friend. You weren't there. To believe in such hatred you need to see it."

Who would be Alexander? Who would be a king if this was the cradle in which kings were formed? And was it for this that lands had to be devastated, great cities thrown down, women bereaved?

"Fathers and sons," I said. "It's an old story. A lot can go wrong."

"And if he wasn't my father? How does that change things?"

"You're not yourself, effendi. You're wounded. You've been hurt."

"I was hurt long before this, my friend."

I spent the night there, sitting beside his pallet in a camp chair. In the morning Alexander instructed me on how to change a dressing. And so it was that I noticed the earlier wounds, the many unsightly scars from which no part of that slender white body had been spared.

"Surprised, my friend? Well, don't be. A god need not be perfect."

"A god, effendi? Did I hear you right?"

"Could a mere man have survived so many affronts?"

Was he joking? Was he feeling better? Was he testing me? Alexander's smile, I knew by now, could mean any number of things.

I haven't mentioned Callisthenes yet, or Apelles. After each new triumph Alexander's artists set to work, Callisthenes with his notebooks and Apelles with his paintpots. Callisthenes collected vivid descriptions of the victory which Apelles illustrated.

Gaza was important not because it was Gaza, I explained to Callisthenes, wanting to make sure that he got things right. Gaza mattered only because it straddled the road to Egypt, a road which now lay open before us.

"Egypt" – Hephaestion always had to get in his own view – "is all dust."

"But just look what they've done with that dust," I persevered.

Alexander, with Egypt next to come, was convalescing even as we marched. Egypt, I warned him, wouldn't fight, by which I meant it wouldn't fight fair. Egypt preferred flattery. It was renowned for its trickery and thus the proverb: Between an Egyptian and a poisonous snake, trust the snake.

Alexander replied with another of his enigmatic smiles.

"So, my friend, we're back to snakes again."

Egypt met us with flowers. I had feared as much. Egypt turned out en masse to welcome Alexander and strew his path with roses.

"Don't be fooled, effendi. It takes only one hand to throw a flower."

"And only one hand to blow a kiss, my friend. I wasn't born yesterday."

We marched on rose petals; we inhaled perfume. Alexander, we learned when we reached the Nile, was to be made a pharaoh. Alexander made a speech in which he protested, briefly, his unworthiness.

He was given another crown, a scroll, and a purple robe. We were shown a camel and a trained baboon. A bellydancer entertained. We were taken then to a river barge, a barge piled high with pillows.

"And where are we supposed to go on this?" Alexander wanted to know.

"Nowhere," Hephaestion fumed. "Nowhere fast."

The Nile, the mighty Nile, the mother of all rivers, surged beneath us. Fellahin toiled along the banks, drawing up water with the most ancient of devices; nearly naked fishermen gracefully cast out their nets. Never before, Alexander remarked, had he been able to look at a landscape with such detachment, without at the same time wondering how he might best deploy his troops.

That night, once we were moored, he asked me to bring him a boy.

"A boy, effendi? What sort of boy?"

"Don't embarrass me, Yusuf. Ask Heff what sort of boy."

Of course I knew perfectly well what sort of boy. That sort of boy was no problem. I made the boy scrub himself first in the river. First an emaciated woman, I was thinking, and now this. I told the boy to leave his clothes piled where he could find them again in the dark – because this time I wouldn't wait up.

Alexander, now dressed as an Egyptian, complete with a tarboosh, stood with the waters of the Nile lapping at his feet, took a deep breath, and slowly filled his lungs with Egypt's hot dry air.

"Can you smell that, Yusuf? Know what it is? The desert."

"Yes it is, effendi. And it has nothing to do with us."

"Oh yes it does, my friend. And the sooner we get started, the sooner we'll get back."

Camels were to be hired. Alexander was adamant. Every container we could lay our hands on was to be filled with water. Against us now would be no human enemy, but merely wave after wave of trackless sand. And his explanation was cryptic.

"Roots, my friend. The big question. Who put me here?"

The sun beat down. Not even Alexander had known a sun like this. First the heat and the flies tormented us and then the lice from the camels, and then a wind began to blow, creating such a storm of dust that we could see neither where we were going nor where we had been.

"Lost," Hephaestion groaned. "Done for. Who can smell the desert now?"

"You're lost only when you panic," Alexander replied coolly. "And we can do without the sarcasm."

Birds were what saved us, dark birds overhead. These birds were a fact, not a miracle. A flock of ravens returning to Siwah, to the very oasis we had set out to find, appeared just in time and led us the remainder of the way with their cries. Date trees rose from the sand, and finally the roof of a temple.

"This is far enough," Alexander ordered. "Wait for me here."

All this way just to wait for him? Alexander unlaced his boots. Like any other petitioner, he had to approach the oracle barefoot, alone, and with his arms full of gifts. Alexander, for once, was no exception.

"Want to bet on it, greaser? Priests aren't stupid. You don't suppose they'll tell him he's not a god, do you?"

"And you?" I said. "What's your opinion?"

"He whipped Darius, didn't he? He taught Tyre a lesson."

"From which you conclude?"

"I don't care, that's what I conclude."

"You don't care whether he's a man or a god?"

"Alexander is Alexander. Who cares what his old lady went to bed with?"

Alexander, striding from the temple, still placed one foot in front of the other. Good news, he said. We had permission to spend the night. He asked me for his writing box but for some time wrote nothing.

The air was still again. The sun was a distant red ball.

"To Olympias from her son Alex, kisses . . ."

I cleared my throat. I wanted his permission to leave. Alexander, like all Greeks, regardless of Plato or Aristotle, could neither read nor write without speaking the words out loud.

"What are you waiting for? Show some initiative. Go and find me a pigeon."

"A pigeon, effendi? There's no need. The cooks are preparing couscous."

"Not to eat, damn you! A carrier pigeon. I want this to go air mail."

And following this Alexander founded a city. Egypt asked if he would, promising that the completed city would always bear his name. Egypt, once again, was to be congratulated; not only was it not to be ravaged but, at Alexander's expense, a city would be built from scratch on what was at present merely a swamp, a morass, a marshland in the delta where the Nile fanned out to enter the sea.

"Well, why not?" Alexander declared.

A few ditches took care of the mud. Dry land began to emerge and Alexander walked over it tirelessly, planning, imagining, pacing everything out beforehand with the architects and the scribes. Barges appeared loaded with stones. Masons turned up, and labourers in papyrus boats; villages appeared overnight along the riverbank and Alexander soon found himself pursued wherever he went by a posse of contractors.

"Can't he see?" Hephaestion complained. "Isn't it obvious? The reason they want us here is so that we can't be any-where else."

Alexander spoke one evening of the two infinities. I was introducing him that night to the hubble-bubble, the hookah, the water pipe, and this was the result. We were caught by these two infinities, Alexander explained, trapped between the greater infinity that was the cosmos and the lesser that was endless division.

"Well that's one way of looking at things," I conceded.

"And is there another way, my friend? What's *your* way?"

Why go in search of trouble? Wasn't the world dangerous enough without that? The world was big enough, I argued, bound by what you could see and what you could count.

"That's a fine trick," Alexander grunted. "For those who can pull it off."

Who would be Alexander? Alexander sucked furiously at the pipe. His tent was strewn with drawings, plans, estimates, all the paraphernalia of yet another battle, a battle against nature herself. Alexander at war was indefatigable.

"And philosophy, effendi? Aristotle, and all that?"

"Have you read him, my friend? Do you know what he teaches? That a whole string of absurdities may be deduced once a single absurdity has been conceded. Try setting that against infinity."

Was Alexander blind? How could I make him see? A city was rising around us, the city of Alexandria. Was that an absurdity? Already the first columns were standing where hitherto only marsh grass had stood, and soon people would be living here. Soon children would be born. They would walk beside their mighty river, stand in the shade of palm trees, gaze out to sea. They would be Alexandrians.

Once more it was Olympias who got him moving. Sometimes two, sometimes three perfumed letters reached us in a single day, and how could logic be set against that? One morning Alexander stepped from his tent, clutching the latest letter, and spoke the words I had been hoping not to hear.

"Tell me, Yusuf. Earn your keep. Which way is India from here?"

"But why, effendi? Just when things seem to be going so well?"

"Are you going to tell me, or do I have to find out for myself?"

The packing began at once. Alexander issued the orders and

Hephaestion passed them on. What he had begun others would have to finish. Instead of a masterpiece, a city of genius, the perfect city of Alexander's imagining, we would be leaving behind a hodgepodge, a miscellany, a sprawl.

In his tent that night, surrounded by boxes and hampers, we were back on wine.

"Nine months' lodging," Alexander joked when the time came to drink to Olympias. "Nine months in the womb and what a price they make us pay."

Always he went too far. Was there only one truth, only his truth? What of my own dear mother, a kindly woman with simple expectations, an ordinary woman sitting on a stool with her legs spread sorting chick peas into the bowl of her skirt?

"Can I speak, effendi? Can I speak freely?"

"Haven't you always, my friend? And don't you still have your tongue?"

"It's just that if I were you, effendi, I would go no further."

"No. You wouldn't. And if I were you, Yusuf, neither would I."

Alexander's drinking, that night, knew no bounds, nor did his bitterness. We toasted Egypt, the sink of all deception. We toasted King Philip, and Philip's catamite, and then we drank to Aristotle, whose meagre philosophy was good enough only for books.

The tent was beginning to spin and I was no longer sure I could walk.

"It's late, effendi. Think of tomorrow. We'll seize tomorrow by the neck and peel it like an orange."

"Yes we will, my friend. We most certainly will. But first fill your glass."

I exchanged a glance with Hephaestion, who also seemed worried. Had we reached the turning point, the watershed, the end of the beginning and the beginning of the end? Alexander was insistent that, as we had drunk to his putative father, we should now drink to Zeus.

We staggered to our feet and we once more raised our glasses.

"And now, effendi, I beg you, draw the line. Quit while you're ahead."

"Sound advice, my friend, except that I'm not ahead."

"Not ahead? Isn't it enough to be a king, effendi, the first of men?"

"Enough to be a king?" Alexander replied with genuine astonishment. "A king enough? To be no more, you mean, than Philip?"

(III)

We saw from the top of a hill that little had changed during our absence, and that Tyre appeared still to be smouldering. Amidst its rubble, however, people were still living, sheltering as best they could, and the smoke, we soon realized, was the smoke from their cooking fires.

Alexander, never so tall as when mounted on Bucephalas, shielded his eyes.

"Not a pretty sight, is it? Not when you think of what was there before."

"Not a pretty sight," Hephaestion echoed. "It never is when you do a job right."

Hephaestion, of course, was wrong. Tyre would rise again, stone would be laid upon stone, orchards would be replanted and terraces restored. If anything was beyond redemption, it was that which carried within itself the seeds of its own destruction. And I pleaded with Alexander one last time.

"Why India, effendi? What's there for you?"

"Precisely, my friend! That's just what I need to find out."

What was India to *me*? Still in the way, moreover, was Darius, who had raised a new army. I waited until the day's march was over, until Alexander had dismounted, before asking his permission to return to my old life.

"Quit, my friend? Now? Just when things are getting interesting?"

"I'm a salesman, effendi, not a soldier. Men, like water, should seek their own level."

"Then seek it and be drowned, damn you!"

That was all. Alexander turned on his heels and disappeared into his tent. This was no way to say goodbye, and I would have gone after him had Hephaestion not placed himself in my way.

"Satisfied now, greaser? You've broken his heart. Somewhere down the road someone's going to have to pay for this."

Hephaestion was what he was. He loved Alexander better than he loved himself. Whether this love was warranted, whether reciprocated or one-sided, and regardless of whether Hephaestion was in any way excused by it, there could seldom have been a more constant love.

The password that evening was "Amazons," but I wasn't tempted.

"So long then," I said to Hephaestion. "Take care. Look after him."

"You bet I will, short-timer. You can read about it in the history books."

Sidon, our own dear city, still intact, was a sight for sore eyes. I approached through the lemon groves. I could smell coffee roasting. I entered the suq at a trot, pushing my way through the evening throng. I could smell mujudra cooking, lentils with rice and plenty of garlic, and I told myself that upon this wide earth there could be no sweeter perfume.

"Yusuf?" my wife exclaimed. "Yusuf Maruf? Fine carpets?"

I would have my work cut out. Somehow I would have to find a way to make this up to her. I greeted my wife and embraced our two dear children, whose hair was full of sand.

"They go to the beach every day, don't they," my wife said.

All of the children did. It was a sign of the times, my wife said. The whole tribe of children was out of control and went running off to the beach first thing every morning to see if any more dead bodies had washed up from Tyre.

Alexander, at their second meeting, made short work of Darius. The news travelled fast. Darius was dead, his army had been beaten all ends up and dispersed, and Persia, once mighty Persia, would now have its mail routed through Greece.

We did an inventory. It was high time. We closed the shop for half a day.

"He'll be thinking ahead now," I said. "He'll already have the maps spread."

My wife was trying to count. She liked doing inventory, liked to find out for herself exactly how things stood. She frowned.

"We haven't sold a single one of these from Baluchistan."

Alexander, we heard, had taken a mistress. Then we heard that he had passed her on to the artist Apelles, who had fallen in love while painting her in the nude.

"Now there's a fine example," my wife remarked, "to set before the world."

We reopened the shop with a sale, to clear out the old stock. Alexander was a conqueror first and last, I explained to my wife. He possessed nothing, coveted nothing. His desires were as simple as they were brief. His vision was of a world at his feet, not in his strongbox and certainly not in his bed.

I got up early one morning and went with the children to the beach. The trick with children was to turn their natural delight in warfare and its cruelty into something more constructive. On the beach I placed a rock in the water to represent the city of Tyre.

"Think now. Suppose you two were Alexander. How would you proceed?"

They stared at me, perplexed. It was clear that they preferred their own games. I felt like banging their heads together.

"Try! Concentrate. Here's a hint. What's the shortest distance from A to B?"

Alexander, drunk, in Samarkand, we heard next, had killed a man with his bare hands. Why? What was happening? Since turning east, Alexander had enjoyed nothing but triumphs. That night I dreamt that there were hands around my own throat. I smelled the wine, his sweat. Afterwards, when I should have been dead, I found myself experiencing his remorse, his grief, Alexander's anguish as he came to his senses and realized that the lifeless body being carried out was mine.

I woke my wife; I asked her to check my neck for bruises.

"It's nothing, Yusuf. Go back to sleep. It's just nerves."

"It's not nothing. Nerves aren't nothing. Light a lamp."

In Bactria, at a symposium, during another drinking bout, Alexander was for the first time worshipped as a deity by the celebrants. Only the historian Callisthenes refused Alexander this honour. Callisthenes knew too much of history for his own good, too little of theology. The next news was that he had been arrested on the charge of plotting against Alexander, a crime for which there had only ever been one punishment.

Alexander, in India, was Alexander writ large. Greeted in Egypt as the rising of another Nile, he was greeted now by the Indians as a Dionysus returning. We heard stories of Pygmies, of husbandless Amazons, of the dreaded Dogmen; we heard how Alexander had survived a close call with a poisoned princess.

"Where there's life there's hope," I said. "Perhaps India's where he'll find himself."

"Are you dreaming when you're awake now too?" my wife said.

At the River of Honey, Alexander came face to face with the Gymnosophists, the Naked Philosophers. And when everything had been conquered by him, the Naked Philosophers asked Alexander, when he had finished seizing everything, where would he take it?

"I'll tell you what I'll do," Alexander said. "I'll cross that bridge when I come to it."

What could stop him? What, now, would prevent him from reaching the end of the earth? Upon the death of his beloved horse Bucephalas, he paused long enough to found another city, the city of Bucephala. Ferocious and unforgiving when it came to punishing those who opposed him, Alexander was equally prodigal in rewarding loyalty.

The letter came from Bucephala, his first letter and the last.

"From Alex the god to his pimp Yusuf, greetings!"

The writing sprawled messily over the page and there were smudges where wine had spilled. There was also a roughly drawn map, with an "x" to mark the spot where he had buried Bucephalas, he claimed, with his own hands.

"The damn thing just packed up on me. That's an animal for you. Well, I've survived worse things, my friend, believe me."

The letter rambled on. His next stop would be the Oxus, a river, but the soldiers were becoming mutinous. Would they really balk at crossing a river, Alexander wondered, when once he would have had only to ask and they would have marched behind him, hay foot straw foot, into the sea?

A few lines were illegible, after which he was speaking again of Egypt, of the past, of Siwah and the desert oracle. He had been allowed, Alexander complained, only a single question about his origin. The priests had recited certain incantations and thrown some substance into the fire to produce a perfumed smoke, upon which the oracle had given out its reply – that the gods themselves had once been men.

"Bloody priests! Was I any the wiser? If the gods were once men, that cuts both ways."

Another wine spill. Whatever the stain obscured was obscured forever. There then followed, at the bottom of the parchment, what – so far as I was concerned – would be Alexander's last words.

". . . still to come? Hard to say. Mother's fine. Wish me well?"

Hephaestion was the next to go. Hephaestion, like Bucephalas, when he had taken as much as he could take, simply lay down. Alexander, we heard, was inconsolable and remained sprawled atop the corpse for days and nights weeping.

The rest followed inexorably, like Aristotle's string of absurdities. The army voted to a man to turn around. The bubble had burst. Alexander, for the first time in his life, was in retreat, forced back not by an enemy but by the very men whose fortitude had once made it incumbent upon him to advance. And so it happened that the news of Alexander's death, when it came, came from Babylon.

I grieved, of course I did. I was no Aristotle, I was no philosopher. I believed in accepting the inevitable, but not stoically.

"I'm sorry too," my wife said. "But I'm only sorry because you're sorry."

On the day that the sarcophagus was to pass, we closed the shop early. We took the children out of school. This was history. Already crowds lined the route. The sarcophagus was housed in a small temple, Doric, on wheels, roofed in gold and pulled by mules, brought from Babylon and now on its way to distant Alexandria, preceded by roadbuilders.

While some threw flowers, others wept, and others still, overcome by their grief, attempted to throw themselves beneath the slow-moving wheels. Here, then, was the final absurdity: here we saw revealed once and for all how, from the ruins of a man, a god might arise.

A woman walked behind dressed in black.

"It's her I feel sorry for," my wife said.

This would be Roxanne, the Persian princess, a daughter of Darius. Briefly the wife of Alexander, she was now already his widow.

"She couldn't have known," my wife said, "what she was letting herself in for."

No one knew, not with a god. A god left nothing and no one undisturbed. The sky opened for a moment, and the light streamed through, and you would never forget that afterwards, never forgive yourself for having seen.

"Shall we go?" I said. "We can still beat the rush."

The small procession having moved past, there was no more to see. The show was over, the apotheosis complete. Our children, those two wild animals, ran on ahead.

"That poor woman," my wife said.

LEAH POSTMAN

Being Famous

Kevin's already in the back room when I get to work at the store. He's eating cereal, holding the bowl over his white shirt. He's got his legs on the table, feet in shiny navy silk socks, no pants on. It makes me happy to see him.

"Sit up straight," I tell him. "You're going to spill on your shirt." He's beautiful, lounging there like a model. His dark legs are sleek, and the muscles roll along his jaw as he chews. I hang my coat on one of the empty garment racks. The coat is a favourite of mine, navy blue military cut, almost right to the floor. But it's showing its wear, and I've got my eye out for a new one.

"Darling," he says, and sweeps a chair out for me to sit. There's a Starbucks on the table, double latte I'm hoping, his. I grab it and it's hot. I keep standing. The coffee is good, sugary.

"Put some pants on," I say.

"That's my coffee," he says.

"Look," I tell him, spreading a free hand on the table. My manicure.

"Very nice." He inspects my fingers one by one, still chewing. The nails are pink and translucent as chiffon, with white tips. Not a cuticle in sight. Kevin spreads his own hand next to mine, and it is huge and square, shiny nails and silver rings. Well-groomed hands are a personal interest of his.

"Lucy?" he asks.

"Esther," I say.

"Ah," he says, nodding. The nail place is a secret of Kevin's – Fancy Nails it's called, but it's not so fancy. It's tucked away in the tiny mall under the bank, coming up from the parkade. The walls are lime green, with fluorescent lights and magazine pictures of Asian and Black women displaying nail fashion: diamond insets, the American flag, beach landscapes. But they do good work there; the manicurists are fast and quiet. I haven't said anything to anyone; I keep Kevin's secret between us.

Tattie and Lola troop in. I remove my hands from the table, from where they are with Kevin's hands, quickly. Who knows what gets said around this place. Lola is rock-hard as usual; Lola, a stripper's name. She works lingerie and she's good at it. Her coat goes over the garment rack, her purse flung onto the small couch. An armful of magazines go on the table. She takes a shiny gold compact out of her pocket and sits down at the table, slicking on skin-coloured lipstick.

"Did you see?" she asks, smacking her lips. Her hair is red, the way it looks on the box in the drugstore. She lights a cigarette, drags deeply. "Show them, Tattie." Kevin's up and putting on his pants, his string tie, his navy silk suit that buttons almost to his collarbone.

Tattie pulls a thick magazine from the pile, and I know it without having to see. I've already got it. Tattie's hands are white and thin as skim milk. Her nails are bitten right down.

"Cold?" I ask. She looks like she's wearing something of her mother's, a floral skirt and pink sweater too long and too big. She's not wearing any makeup and she shrugs her shoulders and arms up and close to her body, fingertips clutching at her sleeve-ends.

"What do we make of this?" Lola's tapping a long beige nail on the cover. It's Suzanna's face, a full shot of her actually, wearing an oxblood fake fur, matching suede pants and a little pink shirt. She's blonde as ever, blue-eyed, tiny little teeth. She's not a model, she's an actress; the full story's on the inside. She's always been way too short, of course, but that hasn't bothered anybody yet.

"She's beautiful?" Tattie volunteers, as though Lola was asking for the one correct answer. Lola studies her a moment, blows smoke.

"Her name was Lola . . . ," Kevin sings under his breath. "We know the story, Lola." Lola stands up fast, does a turn about the room, smoking.

"Five minutes," she says, like she's our boss, like she's our dad giving us fair warning. She's got her arms on her hips, arms akimbo like some siren on the cover of a romance novel. So full-blooded she's about to pop. But I know her secret. I've seen the inside of her purse, her makeup bag a smeary mess of foundation and powders and spilled nail polish, her diaphragm out of its box and cupping lifesavers, a brush full of hair. She's a dirty girl.

Something pokes me in the back.

"Hair," Lola says, pulling a long one from me. She squints at my grey suit.

"Good," she says, "this always looks good on you." It should. It's one of the only things I've got left to wear. But I'm not saying anything.

"Did you see the pictures? Do you think it could have been you? Do you ever think that?"

"I don't know," I say to her. "What are your thoughts?"

"I've got her phone number, you know."

"Say 'hi' from me," Kevin says, waving his hands fast and silly.

She lets go my solitary hair. We watch it fall to the cement floor.

"What's she really like?" Tattie says.

"Hey," Kevin says with exclamation marks all over his voice, "let's call her and find out." Tattie looks at him and she thinks he's being serious. From a distance the silver clasp of his tie looks like a cow skull, strictly country and western. Closer, it's still a cow's skull, but also a human skull, screaming. Lola's back at the table, butting out her cigarette. She shoves her compact in her pocket, smears her lips together in Kevin's direction.

We watch her exit.

"This always looks good on you," Kevin mimics.

"Nice," I say, touching his tie clasp.

"Gaultier," he says.

"Saving your pennies." I'm impressed. "Gaultier," I say to Tattie, who strains to see.

He swigs coffee and smokes his cigarette and we stand there, handing the cigarette off to each other. He tucks a strand of hair behind my ear, neatens up my eyeshadow with his finger.

"Okay?" I say.

"Okay." In her chair, Tattie huddles, her knees up to her chin, and I swear she's shivering. Her small fingers flip through the magazine and Suzanna dances on the page, dressed to the nines in other people's clothes.

One of the first pieces I ever bought was a Calvin Klein silk blouse. I never wore it and it's gone now. It was a simple piece, short-sleeved and snug-fitting, with tiny pearl buttons. The fabric was heavy, a dull white, suggesting a larger, more luxurious garment; I like that. A clean piece, essential in cut, classically minimalist: harbinger of a coming sensibility. I bought it in 1979; I was sixteen. I knew, even then, that it was important. I could smell it, right from the pages of magazines and newspapers, lurking downtown in important stores. I also had an original Halston, a 1977 red tie-around sheath made of silk jersey. I was invited to a party once – a client I had assisted in smaller and larger ways – and found myself in the large closet of the large bedroom of the very large house of the by-then-very-drunk client, who flung garments at me. I'm cleaning house, she kept saying. I think the party was because she had just gotten divorced. I like to think I somehow rescued that dress (along with the Sergio Reid leather shirt and Gucci purse with sunglasses inside and a datebook from 1973, with a French address on the inside cover and a phone number on December 11). The woman whose party it was never mentioned it, later, when she came by the store – didn't remember, I'm guessing, didn't miss a thing. I'm always surprised how little people care about their clothes. For most, I think it's like dressing in paper cutouts of clothes, rather than in the clothes themselves, they care so little about the substance of their appearance. By which I mean the history in the image, some display of meaning: what kind of girl I am, or boy, or where I live or what I do. What breed my dog is, or where I went on vacation the summer I was twelve. Was it the beach or the mountains? Disneyland or the kitchen sink dripping endlessly in an empty house? – specificity is so difficult, which makes easy the seduction of the next new thing.

I sent a thank you note. For the party, of course. I make it a point to be specific.

I talk to Tattie about colour while we're folding sweaters. The sweaters are lovely, skinny silk and cashmere blends, ribbed V-necks in brown and black and blue.

"What would you call this, do you think?" I ask Tattie. She looks scared, bank teller to my bank robber.

"Brown," she says.

"Yes, of course." We keep folding. "What kind of brown, do you think."

She leans against the display table, slumping, as though playing dead might help. She has pale, fine hair clipped flat to her head in a metal barrette. "Um. Chocolate?"

"Yes. Umhum. I was thinking maybe deep hazel. Can you see the green in it?" She nods, frowning at the sweater. Positive encouragement is the key here, I'm thinking. I haven't yet got her on my side. I pick up another one.

"What about this, do you think? Navy, maybe?"

"Um." I've got her thinking. "Yeah. It's a deep . . . blue. Almost black. Black blue." She's trying.

"French navy, really, I would call it. Traditional. Traditional navy has a strong black background. I was reading where the designer chose military colours for this line, abstracting them out, though. Pure colour." Tattie is nodding and folding, folding. "You wouldn't necessarily recognize the camouflage here, don't you think, but it's there." You wouldn't think it, but I hired her myself. Her clothes are awful but expensive. She's been to Europe – for two weeks, a high-school graduation gift – but still, she's been. She looks at the details of things, I catch her studying seams and sleeves and shoes. She just needs the right information.

We finish with the sweaters, and I get her tidying. This is a good place for her to start, the Jil Sander boutique. It's so white and spare it looks as if half the clothes are missing. I like this, things pared back to bone. Once I saved and bought her camel-hair overcoat, when she first came on the scene in 1986. It defined the camel coat, I thought, straight and long with pinched shoulders and slash pockets, like an architect's drawing.

I never wore it. It was stolen.

Down the hall I can hear footsteps running on the hardwood floor, a squeal and a crashing sound – a door slamming maybe, or a large box falling. Tattie looks at me.

I go to the front and look down the hall. It's quiet, there's no one, it's still too early in the morning. The upstairs of the store is designed like a mall, in the grand sense I take it, a public concourse. The hallway runs down the middle, with boutiques on either side, shoes at one end and an open area at the other, where we have the less expensive lines, younger things. There are three boutique sections running down the left side of the hall – the side I manage – linked by arches in the walls. I look through the row of arches, right down to the open area, but nothing's amiss. The two other girls I've got working are invisible; all's quiet.

Kevin appears, at the far end through the arches. He stands like a soldier, hands behind his back. A tall dark-haired woman crosses in front of him, a customer maybe. I can't tell if she's trying something on or just admiring herself; she's standing in front of a mirror.

"You should get Kevin to do your makeup sometime," I tell Tattie. She's got the hangers going the wrong way, and I start to change them. "This way," I say, "facing in and front."

"Is he gay?" Tattie asks.

"Because he's good at makeup?" I keep changing the hangers, but she's not helping.

"I don't know."

"I don't know either." I've seen his legs in my own bathroom in the morning, that dark scalp bent over a bowl of cereal at my own kitchen table; and Suzanna, always so sure, drinking coffee and wearing a T-shirt and my Natori Chinese mules. "I don't know, maybe." Suzanna had a way of getting everyone over on her side.

"Can I borrow a couple bucks?" Tattie asks. She drags her hand along the row of hangers. I ask her for what.

"I wouldn't mind a coffee, is that okay?"

I look at my watch: 10:30. "We've only been here half an hour."

"I know." She's bored. She bunches the clothes on their hangers together, pushes them apart.

"Stand up straight, Tattie."

"What colour would you call this?" She holds out her hands to me and they're covered in a black residue from the metal hanger heads. She's bored, is what I'm thinking, she's mad at me. I suggest she go and work on the inventory sheets. I don't want her getting the clothes dirty.

She slouches to the cash desk, rubbing her hands on her skirt. The first time she did inventory sheets I didn't know what stock had gone out, what was on the floor. It's really my job, but I think responsibility builds confidence.

Anyway, I've got someone to blame if things go wrong.

There's a suit here that looks like me. It's a pantsuit, a liver-coloured satin with skinny slacks and a wraparound jacket. Great with a white T-shirt and loafers. It costs the earth, and I am nowhere near acquiring it, even with my discount, not with everything else I need first. Getting the good stuff takes time, and I figure I lost fifteen years of the good stuff, more if I include the vintage pieces. I've got this grey Donna Karan suit that's at least six years old, another old Demage suit (it's pink, for god-sakes, with shoulder pads), and some black pants. The first thing I had to buy was a white dress blouse, really all I had left was T-shirts and bras. At least my shoes were left; at least we weren't a perfect match.

For two years, I saw Suzanna all over the world in my clothes. There were pictures in magazines of her shooting in Spain where she's got on my Ralph Lauren white cotton men's shirt and wide-legged linen pants, wheat-coloured. The shoes are hers but the sunglasses are mine, wide-arm Opticana Silhouettes that I ate peanut butter for two-and-a-half months to purchase.

In Colorado, at a film festival, she's got on black knit stretch pants, Galliano, and a halter top made out of a ski sweater, also Galliano, red. It was from his "Barbie Goes Skiing" collection, the winter collection that included the parka wedding dress and his reprise of toe socks. Distinctive, controversial, sure to be remembered, definitely worth having. And the Fortuny silk – peach-coloured, like flavoured water. She wore it to the Golden Globes, her hair braided and upswept, like some piece of Grecian statuary. I guess I could be grateful that she appeared to be treating the clothes well, that she was enjoying them. I guess I could be grateful that she thought enough of me to take my clothes. She didn't take money, or my car. She didn't leave behind hidden bills I might have to pay; she left me a cheque for the rent. She became famous in my clothes, but looking at her you know more about me, more about the art director who chooses clothes for a fashion layout, more about the costume designer on any movie than about Suzanna herself. Which is what convinced me she's more a liar than a thief. She's like one of those lizards that changes to match the background except, where she's at, the lizard's the one in front of the camera.

So this is me being famous: Suzanna on TV, laughing and shaking her hair over her face. It is longer and blonder than I've ever seen it. There's a sudden cut to a clip from her new movie. She's holding a gun and shooting, while jumping out a window. There's a huge fireball explosion behind her. Glass cascades around her and she's yelling. I notice her hair is brown, she's got dirt on her face, so I guess this is meant to be serious. A man catches her, his shirt is ripped, and they kiss. The picture cuts back to her, and Suzanna is laughing, laughing. The brown suit she's wearing looks very familiar, like something I once had, like something she took. She could be me, sitting there, on TV, wearing my clothes.

"Tattie," I say. I'm still holding the satin suit. "Tattie, try this on." Tattie looks up from where she's scribbling behind the desk. On the wall behind her is a glass shelf holding a row of glass bottles, each with one white hydrangea bloom. "Just for fun." I walk up to the desk, lay the clothes across the glass counter. She's chewing at a cuticle.

"Don't do that," I tell her. I think of sending her down to Esther for a brand-new set of acrylics. "Let's see this on."

"Coffee," she says, fondling the collar of the suit.

"My treat," I say. "In a minute."

"No," she says. "The colour of it."

"Oh." A good try. But she's not seeing the pink undertones.

The dressing rooms here are large but warmly lit and comfy as a bedroom. There's a little table with a little white vase of white flowers and a white chaise longue. The floors are wood, like the rest of the store, but here there's a Chinese rug, deep green and black. There's a small mirror but only for touch-ups, not full length. It smells like jasmine. Once I slept in here and it was just like staying in a hotel, nicer than anyplace else I had ever been.

"I'll get you some shoes," I let Tattie know.

In shoes, there are boxes spilled all over the floor and the shoes scattered about. I think this was the sound we heard earlier. Someone is on the floor, trying to tidy them, and Lola is standing guard.

"Accident," says the person on the floor. It's Paolo, the new boy. He doesn't realize I'm not a customer.

I grab a pair of strappy stilettos, brushing Paolo's shoulder. He smells good, like something green.

"We've got a guest," Lola says. She's grim, and looks like she's been running.

"Don't mind me," I say, but Lola just looks at me as if she's trying to figure out if I'm actually there.

I see the guest as I'm coming back down the hall. It's someone everyone knows: I can see the famous snake tattoo running up his neck. I know what Lola's doing up here. She has a way of sniffing these things out. There's a tall, dark-haired girl trailing behind him, the same girl Kevin was watching. The Girlfriend. She's got the dreamy look of someone with money to spend; he's got dark glasses on and a long leather coat. He's chewing gum in that smartass way. His shoulders droop.

I duck back into the Sander boutique.

"Let's see, Tattie." She sneaks her head around the drapery.

"I need a T-shirt, or a camisole. I'm naked."

"You can wear the jacket like that, bare. See if these help." I give her the shoes.

Tattie steps out and I'm glad, glad to see what I thought was there has definite potential to emerge. She must be almost six feet in the heels, and her skin is white. She's standing straighter, if only not to expose herself in the jacket. Against her skin, the suit looks almost purple, the colour of veins. I grab her hand and lead her to the three-way.

"I've got a manicure secret I'll let you in on," I tell her. "You've just got to promise to keep it to yourself." She's happy looking at herself, I can tell. I think she's surprised. This is something Kevin's got to see.

Suzanna called me once, late, I think to apologize.

"I'm in France," she whispered. The television was on loud in the background, and I could hear water running.

I asked her if she was crying.

"I don't know," she said, still whispering. There was the sound of a buzzer, and then the sound of Suzanna dropping the phone. I could hear voices but I couldn't tell if they were French or English. She came back on the line and said, hello hello, loudly.

"I'm still here," I said, and she swore. But she didn't hang up. I told her a story then, I think, about a small girl who goes to play with her friend up the street. Her friend has lots of pretty things, pretty dresses and dolls in a pretty pink bedroom. She lives in a house with thick carpeting that has always just been vacuumed. One day the friend shows the girl a ring she got as a prize at a party. The ring is big, with loops of gold piled high like a flower, with a shiny stone in the middle. The girl wants this ring, and when her friend leaves the room she takes it. She takes it home and hides it away in the only pretty thing she has, a small beaded purse. Until another day when the girl comes home and her mother is searching through the house, looking for money, and she has found the purse and empties it on the table, and there is the ring but no money, and her mother is angry and says, "What is this, where did you get this?" and folds the ring into her hand where it is lost. And the lesson, the one she needed to be told, is no matter how much you hide, you will always be found out if you take what isn't yours.

But that's not the real lesson at all. The real lesson, of course, is that what you think is truly yours usually belongs to someone else. But it doesn't matter because I don't think I told her the story then, it was just something I remembered at that moment.

"I have no regrets that I know of," she said. There was a man's voice, calling her name.

"Where are you?" I asked.

"I can't tell," she said. "I just couldn't say." I couldn't imagine, either. I've never been to where she lives.

In the mirror, Tattie looks like a model. Her full name is Tatiana, of course, which is usually ridiculous. But now I'm seeing how she might use it.

"Beautiful," Kevin says. He raises his eyebrows at me. "Needs lipstick." And he's fixing her face, and she's standing there taking it like a pro. "We could have our own fashion show," he says. "Honey, you could walk the hall like a runway. Sell some clothes. Impress the guests."

We three are all clustered in the mirror, three-way times three. It's like we're standing before some sort of pool, and if we just clasp hands and jump there are infinite worlds we might surface in.

"This is like something you used to wear," Kevin says to me, and immediately he looks sorry. "Something you would wear. Would." And I know I don't look right; I know I'm not myself. Maybe I should have tried on the suit, but that opportunity's been taken. I think of all my good clothes, the D&G wide-lapel blue pinstripe suit, my couture Perxes, the burgundy fake-fur neck-to-ankle coat and ecru suede wraparound dress, Daryl K. Everything that Suzanna took. Everything that I gave to her.

Behind us, another figure appears, with the head of a snake. I step out of the mirror, maybe to assist him with a purchase, maybe to give him a better view. I might as well be naked; I disappear. My hands are clasped together, and I don't know where I might appear next.

GEOFFREY BROWN

Listen

Listen to me. Are you listening to me? Listen to me. I want you to listen. You listen. To me.

I tried not to notice. I pretended not to notice. I closed my eyes and didn't notice. I knew what I wasn't noticing. I could hear what I wasn't noticing. I could hear things break. I could hear things rip. I closed my eyes and not noticed. Things broke. Things ripped. I failed to notice.

They arrived prepared. They brought their "tools." Their "instruments." Their "utensils." They arrived and went to work. They worked. They finished. They "put away" their "tools." "Packed away" their "instruments." "Washed off" their "utensils."

One morning there she is. He sees her as he leaves. There she is. He leaves.

I gave myself an hour. I thought, An hour will be plenty. How long is an hour? How much can an hour take? It took an hour. It took longer than an hour.

They knocked on his door. He let them in. Offered coffee. Took them out. Showed them the grounds. "These are the grounds," he said. He waved his hands. Brought them in. They went through the house. Let themselves out. He rinsed the cups.

"Don't do it," I thought. I said it to myself: "Don't do it." I said it out loud. "Don't do it."

I could do anything. Whatever I wanted. Whatever there was.

I was supposed to wait. I made a deal. "I'll wait. I'll wait a week." I made another deal. I couldn't wait a week.

I keep thinking, What will happen? I keep thinking, What will happen if it happens?

I've never done this. I don't know why I'm doing this. I can't imagine why I'd do this.

It happens often. Not all that often. Fairly often. You could almost say it happens fairly often. It often happens fairly. You could almost say it happens fairly often. You couldn't say it happens fairly. I don't think you should say it happens fairly. I don't think you should say it happens. I think it happens. But I don't think you should say it happens.

I keep changing. I can't decide. I change. I decide. I can't decide.

She came over. It was the first time she came over. She came over for the first time and he let her look around. She moved about the room and looked around. He sat in his seat.

I had a plan. I thought I had a plan. I thought I had a plan worked out. I thought I knew the plan I had. I thought I knew the plan I had that I was going to do.

They called me. They told me they were ready. "We're ready," they said. I told them I was ready. I told them I would pick them up. I went to pick them up. I picked them up.

I kept trying. I have no idea why I kept trying. I could never do what I kept trying to do. I kept trying to do what I had never done. Trying to do what I had never done kept me trying.

I had only one. I only had one. I had one only. Only I had one.

This can't be done. I shouldn't do this. I shouldn't be doing this. I can't do this.

I did it one way and then I did it a second way. I put it back the way it was before I did it the first way. I did it a third way. I tried to put it back the way it was the time I did it the second way. I couldn't remember how I did it when I did it the second way.

I was doing it incorrectly. I was doing it wrong. Not the way it said. Not according. I was holding it wrong. I wasn't clutching. I had it wrong.

I told him what to do. I drew a diagram. I showed him. "I understand," he said.

He said, "I want to show you something. Come here."

They went. The two of them. They went ahead. They met with the others. There were others who were there whom they were meeting with. There were others who were waiting. They were waiting.

Inside it was dark. They felt their way along. "Slow down," she said. He stopped.
   "What's wrong?"
   "Don't stop."
   He moved.
   "Come on."

I decided to go. I could have stayed. I could have decided to stay. I could have decided to go. I could have decided. I wasn't being forced. No one said I had to go. No one said: "Go."

I promised I would go. I went. I promised I would go. I went. There was no one there. I promised I would go. I went. There was no one there. I promised I would go. I didn't want to go.

I got it done. I got one done. I still have two to do. No, that's not right. I have as many to do as I haven't done. Of those I've done, there are none I haven't done. Of those I haven't done, I have as many yet to do.

I went back many times. I don't know how many times I went back. I can't remember how many times I went back. I remember going back many times. Numerous times. I went back. I went back. I went back. I went back. More times than that. I came away. I should have stayed.

He went first.
  "Your turn," he said.
  "No. Your turn."
  He went.
  "Your turn," he said.

I liked the way she looked. She said she liked to look. She said she liked to watch. I let her watch. I let her watch a lot. She never asked to touch. She never tried to touch. She only ever looked. I think she liked to look. I think she liked to watch.

No one paid attention. Not to me. No one paid attention to me. They paid me no attention.

I turned around.
  I heard my name. I turned around.
  Someone waved. I couldn't make them out. They waved. I waved back.

I took what I had and went over. I didn't have much. It fit in a bag. It fit in one bag. What it was was what fit in a bag. A bag was all it was. The size of a bag. The it was not without the bag. Without the bag the it it was was not.

I went first. She went second. I went first. She went second. We went one after the other. Me first, her second. First one, then the other. Me, then her.

I wanted to go. I was ready to go. I thought I was ready to go. I felt I was ready to go. I think I was ready to go. I think I thought I was ready to go.

"Listen," she said.
    "Look," she said.
    "Are you ready?" she said.
    "Do you want to?" she said.

He told me he didn't care. I knew for a fact he did. He cared.
    "I know you care."
    "I don't care," he said.
    "You care."
    He cared.

It was easier than he thought. He thought it would be hard. It was hard.

He moved back. He went forward. He stepped back. Stepped forward. It was not a hesitation. I wouldn't say he hesitated. I wouldn't say the stepping back and forth was hesitation. I would hesitate to say the stepping back and forth was not a hesitation.

I like to think that I'm prepared. If being prepared is possible. If being prepared is something for which one can be prepared. I like to think that I'm preparing to prepare.

He held up his hand. "Did you hear that?"
    "Wait," he said. "Stop," he said. "Listen," he said.
    I waited. I stopped. I listened.

ROBERT McGILL

The Stars Are Falling

Tim floated with his mouth just out of the water and his goggles pushed up on his forehead, hyperventilating calmly and gathering himself. The distance of the dock and shore produced a strange peacefulness in him, but it was the kind that at any moment could slip into panic, so that he might thrash about and exhaust himself and drown in eight feet of water. Tim flinched at this thought, sent it drifting and tried to relax his body. Looking down, he could see the white of his underwear against summer-brown skin and, a little to the side, the murky shape of Paul still busy in the search. He would have to come up soon.

"Are Croatians afraid of water or what?" Tim called to the ski boat between breaths. "Come on. The first guy who brings one up gets a case of beer." Andro was still on the deck, wearing a T-shirt that read *"Found Myself In / Bedford Indiana."* The second line looked like it had been printed on separately, evidence that the shirt was being sold in hundreds of versions across the continent. Tacky, Tim thought. The kind of thing people bought in a tourist frenzy and passed off to somebody else at the first opportunity. That was probably what had happened. Andro had probably never even been to Indiana. Tim stared at the shirt, keeping his head low, waiting for Andro to remove it. Then Paul burst through the surface, trying to breathe and shout at the same time and making a sound like an empty drinking-box after being squeezed. He was clutching something in his hand: a fishing lure, still shining and intact. But on the way back to the boat, he caught the hooks in his fingers and Andro had to drag him out by the armpits. He left behind a cloud of blood that faded as slowly as jet vapour.

They'd disturbed the sediment that covered the bottom, and even through goggles the lake-floor was impossible for Tim to see. He went down with his hands in front of him until he felt stone, soft and hard at the same time. The lake was full of these reefs, ice-age relics all running in the same direction. They were carved from a brown rock that you could pull off with your hands. Tim hated the slimy, decomposing texture. He dreaded feeling around blindly while the air staled in his lungs and his brain indexed all the things his hands might touch. It would be better from the boat. With some old glass and wood they could put together a viewfinder to look at the bottom without even getting wet.

He found nothing and kicked to the surface just in time to see Andro jump, still wearing his shirt. Maybe it was a Croatian thing. Then Tim realized that a red aluminum canoe had appeared at the side of the ski boat. The woman in it was talking to Paul. Tim had seen her before; Dana, that was her name. Her hair was a colour more yellow than blonde, and she wore a blue tank-top that showed off the tops of flaccid, liver-spotted breasts. Sitting in the canoe straight-backed, with her sharp nose and her plucked eyebrows, she looked to him like a parody of an Indian princess. Tim began a slow, inept sidestroke towards them but was pulled up short by Paul's voice.

"Andro, what you got there?" A hand reached over the far side of the ski boat and dropped a clump of dripping dirt onto the deck. "Watch it!" cried Paul. "You'll put a hole in the damn boat." But it was a half-hearted rebuke; Paul was already holding the thing in his hand, judging its weight, looking at it from every angle. Andro climbed the ladder at the stern and sat on the side with his feet hanging off, lazily kicking the lake.

"Jesus," breathed Paul. "It looks like a rock. You sure this is one?"

"Give it to me," said Andro. By that time Tim was floating at the side of the canoe, holding on to its rubber coaming. He watched as Andro took the thing out of Paul's hand without hesitation and smashed it against the side – like it was somebody's head. There was a series of plopping sounds as pieces fell into the water and when he pulled the rock back into view it had transformed. One half was the same shape as before, but the other was long, tubular and metallic.

"So the guy wasn't lying after all," said Paul. Dana wanted to know what it was.

"It's a mortar shell," Paul replied. Andro corrected him: it was only part of a shell. A whole one would be dangerous. Paul nodded with his eyes closed, as though this were a fair but unimportant point. Then he repeated what he had been told by the mechanic at the marina: that the army used to own the lake and all the land around it before there were cottages. They sent up soldiers from Trenton for war games and artillery tests. There were still pieces from old shells down at the bottom, if you knew where to look.

Dana seemed unimpressed. She asked for an introduction to the new man.

"This is my cousin Andrija," said Paul. "He's visiting from Croatia for a week." Andro gave a half-wave and smiled obligingly. Dana reminded Paul that she was Croatian, too. "Well then, you should come over to the Pagoda tonight and the two of you can have a chat. I'm throwing a party." Dana nodded when he suggested a time, then pushed off and paddled away.

"Well, there goes one piece of woman," said Paul.

"Who is she?" asked Andro, still fingering the mortar shell.

"The girlfriend of the old guy who owns the A-frame across the lake," replied Tim. "She doesn't talk to people much. Nobody can understand her, anyway, with that accent."

"Her name's Dana," said Paul, licking a bit of blood from his palm. "She's come by a couple of times. I think she's lonely. She's come overseas for the summer and now the bastard's left the province; said it was some kind of emergency business trip, and she's stuck here by herself waiting for him. She's got a kid back home, too."

"How old do you think she is? Thirty-five? Forty?" Andro was thirty-two.

Paul shrugged. "Too old for me and Timmy, that's all I need to know." He looked at Andro slyly. "Why? You interested, maybe?"

"What if I am?"

"Two Croatians, what were the odds?" said Tim with mild sarcasm. "Maybe it was meant to happen."

"Anyhow," said Paul, "we know she puts out." Andro grimaced and did a roll into the water, indicating it was time to resume searching. He found two more, and Paul managed to drag up a small one, too. They stayed longer than Tim would have liked, but he was not going to be the first one to suggest leaving. Worse, he suspected they were waiting for his sake so that he might also find one. He should have been grateful, but his head was throbbing from the sun and heat, and he felt only spite. He was relieved when Paul finally said it was time to go home.

They were halfway to the dock when Andro took off his shirt. Trying to be inconspicuous, Tim looked at Andro's chest, his arms. There were no marks, not even any hair. The only things he could find were two round inoculation scars on a bicep, one above the other like a light socket. That was all. Tim wasn't sure what he had been expecting. Burns, maybe. A tattoo with maps and hieroglyphic code. A chest wound that had never fully healed, one that shrank and grew as Andro breathed. Even that would not have surprised Tim like this blankness. Paul had told him dozens of stories about what the man had been through, stuff to make you sick to your stomach, and here was nothing whatsoever to corroborate them. He was so taken aback that he didn't understand at first when they began to slow, the motor dying in pitch from a shriek to a displeased gurgle. They were coming alongside Dana in her canoe, and Paul was easing the boat by her out of courtesy. She stopped paddling as they passed, and she stared fiercely. Tim's head dropped for a moment in embarrassment, but then he realized that she was not looking at him. She was watching Andro. He was meeting her eyes, not smiling, not even blinking. Paul had also noticed what was happening. He was going to say something about it any moment; he must. But he stayed silent.

Then Paul increased the speed and Andro turned his gaze to the sky.

"Might rain tonight," he said.

Almost twenty people, all of them vacationers, showed up at the Pagoda. That was the name Paul's family had given to their cottage, which was octagonal and sat ten feet above the ground on a central concrete pedestal. When Paul's parents had built it five years ago, they claimed it was a popular style of architecture in California. Other cottagers on the lake complained privately that this was not California. They argued over whether it looked more like a spaceship or an oversized tree fort, and pointed it out to guests when they drove past. Before the hamburgers were served, when everyone was still on their first beer, Andro and the mortar shells were the centre of attention at the Pagoda, temporarily pushing to the periphery the usual discussion of local intrigues. The shells were displayed on the patio picnic table with some towels underneath them, and Andro went through them all in formal lecture style, explaining how they were fired, their ranges, their destructive capabilities, even the noises they made in the air.

"Not like that whistling sound in the movies," he said. "Not when they're coming right at you. More like a bird flapping its wings." People frowned, because this was the appropriate reaction, and because this kind of material had not been expected. It made them nervous. Tim could see some of them searching for a joke, but they were quiet and frustrated, afraid to say the wrong thing. Tim was hungry for someone to ask a stupid question so that they would have a person to pick on. That always solved it, he thought: making another guy feel even smaller than you. Paul was a possible target. He had wrapped his hand ostentatiously in bandages, something a military man might ridicule, and Gillian made a few teasing remarks precisely along those lines. *You're a real tough guy, Paul. Look at those battle wounds.* It was obvious to all of them that she was hoping Andro would join in, but he didn't take the bait.

When Andro had finished they scattered: a few people went to the back yard and tried to start a fire in the pit, while others picked raspberries from the edge of the forest where the crickets were playing. Andro and Dana walked by themselves down the driveway, and Tim watched them from the patio until they vanished behind the trees, Andro touching her arm. Paul appeared and disappeared, busy making sure that things ran smoothly. He had already made four trips to the variety store and in the morning had driven to a farmer's stand out on the highway so that in the bathroom right now a watermelon was cooling in the tub. There was delighted laughter each time someone new went in. Tim wondered if Paul worked so hard because he knew that people didn't like him. They came to the parties for one reason: his money. Or more precisely, his parents' money, and their habit of letting him have the Pagoda to himself. Otherwise he was just another university student with acne scars. Tim felt a sudden pang of guilt. It wasn't kind to think of such things; they were easier to ignore at school in Toronto, when he and Paul were simply friends and he was not a guest.

It was after dark when Andro returned. Everyone had gathered in the dining room, with stripped corn cobs and half-eaten buns around them, to play games: Telephone, Psychiatrist, Magic Numbers, Black Magic. It was funny how many had "magic" in the title. There was always a trick that people had to figure out, and it was supposed to seem like magic until you did. But mostly Tim just felt stupid. He sat on a chair in a corner, conscious of his own smell and angry for having worked too hard lugging firewood. The washer at the Pagoda didn't do a proper job either. It always left clothes smelling as though they had been rinsed in someone else's sweat. Tim sucked on his beer aggressively. When they played Who'd I Shoot? he put his finger to his head as he said "Bang bang bang," and Andro shook his head with a tired smile. Then Gillian came in dragging Dana by the hand.

"Guess what? She's going to tell our fortunes," Gillian said, with a zeal that implied it had taken some convincing. "She has gypsy blood, you know. Her people lived in a caravan and travelled through the mountains in Croatia." Gillian had to be making that up, thought Tim. Dana hadn't told her anything.

When the women were done clearing away the dishes, they clustered around the table and Dana prepared for her performance, urged on by half-drunken incitements. The cards she used were strange, from a deck she had brought from Croatia. Dana called them *baštela*. The suits were exotic and indecipherable: one with coin-like circles, one with shapes that looked a bit like truncheons and one a bit like flower-pots. The fourth was a labyrinthine swirl of lines. She laid them face-down in a grid and began to flip methodically. Two or three were turned over, focused on, and after a few seconds she told them what she had seen.

"Look at her concentration!" laughed Paul. "Gillian, I think you've found the real McCoy. She could've run away from the circus."

Gillian's fortune came first. Dana told her that she would die at the age of sixty-seven. This was accepted with a nod; it was a number without any meaning. Then she said that Gillian would be pregnant six times but have only four children. There was an outburst of disapproval. No, they protested, you couldn't say things like that. There were rules to this kind of game. Predictions could be negotiated. The audience could demand retractions. Dana didn't seem to know these rules existed.

All right, agreed Dana reluctantly. Pregnant six times, though. I'm sure of that.

"Any love in her life?" asked Paul, hoping to bring things back within a comfortable range.

Yes, there was love. No one escapes love.

When Dana declared that Gillian's fortune was finished, someone said that Paul should go next. His face blanched. He mumbled something, then said it louder: he wanted to know if there was a death card. He wouldn't do it if there was a death card. No, assured Dana. It was only a trivial game, for fun. Tim wondered where she had learned the word "trivial."

"All right," said Paul, sitting down across from Dana and clasping his hands together loudly. "How many kids, and how much money will I make? Tell me the important stuff." She shook her head. It wasn't that simple. She could only read what the cards told her. Nevertheless, he ended up satisfied with what she saw: a long life, good sex. She said he was always trying to please people; he needed to do more for himself, expand his horizons. Tim watched Dana flip the cards and listened to what she said. There was no discernible pattern, no predictable reaction to any suit or number.

"It's amazing how much she's gotten right," exclaimed Gillian. "And she doesn't even know any of us." There was something slightly odd about the way Gillian said it, as though Dana weren't even in the room. Tim suspected that Gillian didn't know her name.

"Why don't you do Andro?" Gillian wanted to know. Dana shook her head. Oh no, I couldn't. No, really. No. But Paul had been talking, and everyone knew there might be something between these two. They bullied her. They wouldn't let her leave. All right, she said in the end. I'll do it. Fine. She rearranged the cards, and they made Andro take Paul's place directly opposite her. Then Dana began, never taking her gaze from the cards. It was late and Paul had lit candles around the room. The ceiling fan had blown them out at first so he'd shut if off, and now the house was shadowy and hot.

The seven of *špade*. You value your independence. You have given up caring what other people say or do to influence you. You resent their pressure, and you resist when you feel it applied. You have given up on understanding other people; you want them to stop trying to understand you.

The two of *baštoni*; and the jack. You have been in love before, you will be in love again. Love has always hurt you and now you fear such intimacy, but you expect that it will return sooner or later, probably sooner. The ace of *coppe*. You have hurt people in the past. You worry that you do not feel sorry enough about this, but you would do it again if you were given the choice. This doesn't frighten you. It means you have consistency: a way of holding yourself together.

The jack of *špade*. There has been a woman in your life. She was in a small place that you visited. An affair, in the middle of conflict. People were hurt, killed. You left without saying goodbye. It was many years ago. You never expected you would

see any of them again, not her or parents or sisters. You have forgotten them now. Your hands are clean.

You don't know what you're doing here. You are too far away
from the people you love. The customs are strange. Your real life
seems distant and unreal. You need to go home.

The four of *dinari*. There. That's all. That's all I see.

Dana stood up and left the room. No one else moved. Tim
suddenly wished that they would all go home. He wished that
Andro could be by himself. No, that wasn't true, it was Tim who
wanted to be alone right now, to understand, to make sense. He
could feel around him the imminent release of speculative
energy – silent hypotheses pressing to be spoken – but nothing
would be accomplished through that. Suddenly all the brunt of
the day's sun hit him. He was lightheaded, dizzy. His eyes ached,
his lips felt shrunken into his face. He could feel his nostrils
burning, he could feel *everything*, even the darkness of his own
skin. Not even water would soothe him now; it would only
taste hot and syrupy and suffocate him. He needed to escape to
a pitch-black bedroom and lie down on cool sheets in absolute
quiet. But Paul rocked back on his chair and blew out a mouth-
ful of held air, and that became the signal for everyone to begin.

Was she trying to hurt him? Why? Or did she really see those
things? Who could make up a story like that? Obvious, stupid
questions. None of them really cared about the answers. They
were more interested in the guessing.

"Don't worry," said Paul to Andro. "I'm sure she didn't
mean it."

Andro shrugged. "You Canadians try too hard to be peace-
keepers," he said. Then he got up and left the table. No one tried
to stop him. Without Andro there, they could say even more.

Eventually Paul and a few others got tired of the excitement
and went outside to smoke, but seconds later he returned.

"Hey everybody, the sky is falling," he announced. He was as
drunk as the rest of them and no one paid any attention at first,
but after he explained, word spread quickly around the house.
Meteors. Of course, said Gillian indifferently, it was the Perseids
shower, it happened every year. But the rest had decided that
this was going to mean something and they rushed to the patio.

It was crowded with sprawled bodies until someone had the idea to climb to the roof.

The stars were everywhere, thick and soupy, except on the eerie fringes where the cedars crept into the sky. The only landlocked light came from a few distant dock lamps and the occasional glitter of eyes from the forest. Tim could see the still surface of the lake from up here, too, sparkling with tiny points of light. Lying on his back, he turned his focus to the stars themselves and – every minute or so if you were paying attention, if your peripheral vision was sharp and your reflexes quick – the flickering interpenetration of heaven and earth.

Most people were whispering, although Paul was not; he was improvising a story about what would happen if a meteor landed in the lake. He filled it with tidal waves, dust clouds, and people trapped underground in bomb shelters.

"He doesn't know what he's talking about," said a voice near Tim. It was Andro, lying beside him.

"No, he doesn't," Tim agreed. He struggled for something else to say. "This is spectacular. This is great. You probably don't get a show like this way over there in Croatia."

"Of course we do," Andro grunted. Tim was surprised. Wasn't there a time difference? What about the angle of the earth, the latitude? He stumbled through his sentences, not finding the words he wanted, which was funny, since it was Andro whose first language was not English. But Andro didn't seem to notice. He replied that the entire planet was passing through the tail of a comet. It lasted a few days every year, but you only noticed what was happening at night.

"Sure, sure," said Tim. "I knew all that." He was given a reprieve from further speech by a meteor that flared halfway across the sky to appreciative cheers.

"So you think she was telling the truth?" said Andro, startling him when it was quiet again. Tim hurried to respond just as casually.

"Oh no," he said. "You mean with the fortune, right? Of course I don't. Why? It's not true, is it? I mean, it couldn't be true. You never met any sister."

"I don't know."

"What do you mean? Are you saying it could have happened?"

"Yes." He said it and sighed; too feminine a gesture for Andro, Tim thought. Then Andro began to talk. Everything she had accused him of was so general, so vague. Who was to know? Those kinds of things were happening all the time during the fighting. Lots of guys, lots of women, all of them caught in a bad time. This whole thing now was bad. She was a good woman. They'd been talking earlier, they'd gone for a walk along the old logging road while the others were eating, and they were getting along fine until they broached the subject of the war. He got carried away. He got too specific. He didn't think it would cause any trouble.

"So what are you going to do?" asked Tim.

Andro snorted. "Nothing. What else should I do?"

"I don't know. Go after her."

"No," said Andro. "It's not worth it. I was just seeing how far I could get. I'm gone in a few days and that would have been it."

"I don't believe you," said Tim.

"Fine. Believe what you want."

Tim scanned for meteors but with no success. The sky had gone dead.

"What's it like?" he said at last. It was the question he had wanted to ask for the three days they had been at the Pagoda. "You know. Killing someone." There was silence. After a while he worried. He imagined Andro seething, tensing, preparing to stand up and throw him from the house. But then the voice spoke, slow and quiet.

"It was no big deal, after a while."

"Really?" He tried to swallow but his throat was too dry. "I don't think I could ever bring myself to do something like that."

"You could," said Andro. "Anybody can."

Most of them were still up on the roof when Tim climbed down to the patio. He went to his room, stripped to nothing and lay down on the bed. It was a proper cottage bed with creaking springs and a lumpy, lopsided mattress that threatened to roll him to the floor. It felt out of place in this building. From above came the sound of footsteps and laughter and, once or twice, breaking glass. Tim frowned. Up there had been a different kind of exposure. It left him not fiery and peeling but tired and vacant, as though something were about to blossom in a place where he would never see it.

Then he heard sounds coming from the bathroom on the other side of the wall. The running of tap water; the roll of the toilet paper dispenser; two soft voices. One of them became louder, and Tim realized it was Gillian's, kind and harsh and condescending at the same time. *It's all right now. He's up on the roof with the rest. Pull yourself together.*

In the mind's eye of sleep, Tim is still at the party. The guests are all inside the Pagoda and the lights are on, but outside it is absolutely dark. The windows are closed and the ceiling fan is thrumming as it turns. Tim is looking for Andro and Dana, but he can see neither of them. He searches the entire house, even the closets and cupboards, under the beds. No sign. He is afraid that he will have to go outside by himself to find them. Animal eyes watch through the windows. Then Tim awakens and begins the administrative task of sorting dream from reality. He is still uncertain about some things when he hears again the knocking that awoke him and he sees Andro standing in the doorway.

"Get up. Come with me. We are going after her."

Tim dresses and they pass silently through the house. There is someone asleep on the couch, anonymous within the ruffle of a sleeping bag, but otherwise the Pagoda is deserted. The stairs and the ground below them are littered with beer cans, bottles, an ash tray. It is not yet dawn. In the time it takes them to walk the driveway, Andro tells him what Gillian has said: that Dana left in the darkness sometime after four. She said she was going home in the canoe. The A-frame does not have a telephone and Gillian is worried. The implication is clear: We are doing this for Gillian. We are not doing this because of me.

The path to the lake is rocky and slick with dew. Andro walks silently, and Tim thinks that he must be preparing himself for some great rescue. Strangling rattlesnakes in his hand, or mouth-to-mouth resuscitation. After all, that is what Tim is imagining. But they arrive at the dock and they can see her canoe pulled up on the far shore. The lake is too narrow to permit much fantasy.

The A-frame is over there waiting for them dark and lonely, nestled in fairy-tale forest. There is not a breath of wind, and the water sits smooth and reflecting morning colours. The motor is sleepy and slow to start. Tim has been instructed in operating the boat, but Paul usually insists on driving and Tim does not have much experience. Finally it is Andro who knows what to do with the gas tanks, squeezing tubes and loosening caps. He takes the wheel and guides them away from the dock.

Halfway across the lake, Tim calls out for Andro to slow down. Something is floating in the water. Tim goes to the bow and reaches with the net, brings it back and fishes out the object with his hand. It is a playing card.

"Look," he says, pointing not to the card but to the lake.

They are lying flat and motionless ahead of the boat: the *baštela* cards, in a long trail that suggests they were not scattered all at once but set down deliberately, one by one. The sun has just begun to edge over the trees and makes them flash like knives. They are spaced so evenly that if you were quick enough and light enough, you could hop from one to the other all the way across the lake. An invitation or a warning: from this distance it is impossible to tell.

The two of them go along slowly, Tim at the bow with the net and calling directions to Andro, veering and scooping them out, until they have half the pack. They begin to weave around to pick up strays. Sometimes Tim fumbles and misses one, or Andro speeds up at the wrong time, and soon enough they are laughing and flinging water from bailing buckets and calling each other assholes. With the sun up, nothing seems serious anymore. In the back of Tim's mind he remembers where they are going, but he and Andro are following a mutual impulse, an instinct for play, until finally they are pushing at the jagged edges of the lake where the reeds cluster south of the cottage, ready to choke an engine. They are so much into their own game that they have forgotten all the other rules, and Andro almost drives right onto shore. Tim has to yell at him to stop.

They drift at the side of the vegetation, both suddenly confused. There is a compulsion to do something, anything to accelerate the game, but they seem trapped. A second later and the laughter and exhilaration will be irrecoverably gone. These need to be perpetuated, climaxed, if just for a second. Tim can only think of one thing. He throws all the cards over the side of the boat with a single swing of the arm.

Three or four make it as far as the reeds, but most of them catch on the air and flutter down in front of him, a few landing on the deck. Tim's gut flips with unfulfillment. He picks up the cards at his feet and throws them overboard again. One of them stubbornly falls back into the boat, and he swipes it viciously from the wet fibreglass, crumples it and hurls it away.

He turns, breathing quick and shallow, and freezes. Andro has been watching him silently. But with Tim's eyes on him, Andro starts to laugh: a low chuckle from the back of his throat, like he's been waiting for Tim to do that, as though Andro has kept his head and known the right thing to do all along. Tim recognizes that laugh. It's the way that you are supposed to finish such games. It's the way you win.

NEIL SMITH

Green Fluorescent Protein

The human genome is what Ruby-Doo is babbling about. The two of us are in Westmount Park. I'm practising my hook shots as he slumps on a bench alongside the basketball court.

Ruby-Doo has, what else, a book in his hands. He's a short-ish, skinnyish guy. Well, at least compared with me.

"Wouldn't it be incredible," he says, scratching his armpit, "to map the thousands of genes in your body? Track down where each one comes from. Discover hidden traits."

Yesterday, his mother told me Ruby-Doo is a gifted child. But isn't gifted *child* an insult at seventeen? I'm seventeen too. One of my biggest gifts: twirling a b-ball on my index finger.

I sink the ball from half-court, and Ruby-Doo does the fake crowd roar – the hushed wahhhh – I taught him. I dribble over to his bench.

"Say you harbour the gene to become a musical prodigy," he says, blinking in the July sun. "Except you're totally unaware because you've never sat down at a piano. Unlike dwarfism or red hair, musical genius isn't visible. You see it only under special conditions."

In a field beside the courts, a theatre troupe is rehearsing *Romeo and Juliet*. Every now and then, Ruby-Doo is drowned out by some goof in tights yelling "Prodigious birth of love it is to me!" or something equally lame. But Ruby-Doo doesn't seem to notice; he rattles on about certain genes being top-secret files we need special security clearance to open. I remember my mom saying that alcoholism is hereditary and that maybe she and I both have the gene, so I tell Ruby-Doo I don't want to open those secret files.

"Probably bad news," I say.

Ruby-Doo eyes me like he's working on a science report on today's average teenager. "You know, Hippie," he says, "sometimes you're a real naysayer."

What the hell's a naysayer?

"Piss off," I say.

My real name is Max. Hippie is what Ruby-Doo calls me. The nickname is a joke: I have a buzz cut, wear polo shirts with little alligator logos, and play on a basketball team. I call René-Louis Robidoux by his last name, pronouncing it like Scooby-Doo. We met at the start of the summer when my mom and I moved to Westmount from Saint-Bruno.

Every afternoon while I was shooting baskets, Ruby-Doo would be in the park reading. He always looked so absorbed; it bugged me. One day, I deliberately shot the ball at him, knocking his book flying.

Apologizing, I went and picked up the book and dusted it off. On the cover was the whiskered mug of a monkey. "What's your book about?" I asked, handing it over.

The Third Chimpanzee, he said, was about evolution and genetics, about the development of language and art.

"And also about sexuality," he added.

"Sexuality?"

"Yeah, like why women can't tell when they're ovulating," he said, straight-faced. "Like why men have such long dicks but such small balls compared with chimps."

I held the b-ball to my hip.

"You're kidding, right?"

His mouth curled into a grin. That's when I noticed his eyes: one was brownish, the other blue. Just like some Alaskan huskies you see.

My mom and I moved to Westmount as part of her Life Overhaul. She wanted everything new. New job: as a partner in a private dermatology clinic. New boyfriend: a dweeb anesthesiologist named Brian who calls me Sport and sucks on toothpicks in public. New hair dye: something called Peruvian Fire (looks like the colour of barbecue chips). New AA group: the Westmount chapter, which she goes to every week.

Our new home is the top floor of this big brick house around the corner from the YMCA. The apartment has a wicked long hallway, like a bowling alley of blond wood. Another cool thing: the private bathroom off my bedroom has a fancy stained-glass window that makes taking a leak a religious experience.

One night, I get home from Passion des Fruits – the grocery store where I stack produce part-time – and find my mom sprucing up for a date. She frowns at herself in a hallway mirror. "These canine teeth of mine," she says, "stick out like box seats at the opera."

While poking in her clunky earrings, she asks whether Brian reminds me of my dad: "You know, the bear chest, the pointy chin."

"Maybe," I say. "Except Brian isn't some dead stiff whose widow is already screwing around."

My mom turns the colour of her hair. "You little shit," she spits out. "Don't you tell me how to grieve."

"Ma, I'm only joking," I lie.

She throws an earring at me. Misses me by a mile.

Two years and two months ago, my dad died of a brain aneurysm. Just dropped dead on the curling rink while lining up a shot. He was a big curler, my dad. He once joked he'd like his ashes placed in a hollowed-out curling stone.

Guess what – my mom decided to do it.

"For cripe's sake, he was only kidding!" I shouted and then burst into these weird yelping sobs. My mom grabbed me by the shoulders, pressing so hard my tears instantly stopped. "Listen to me, Max," she said in a freaky yell-whisper. "We all need a little levity. You understand me?"

I didn't argue. I didn't want to stress her out even more because in times of stress she'd often drop in on her old cronies Margarita and Bloody Mary. Two weeks after the funeral, I found her in the kitchen, pale and shaky. In her hands was a two-arm corkscrew contraption, like something you'd abort a fetus with.

"Whatcha doing, Ma?" My voice sounded small and babyish. Scared.

"Nothing, honey," she mumbled.

That's when I saw the bottle of white wine on the counter. I stood in the doorway, watching her uncork her bottle, pour a glass, and dump the rest – *clug, clug, clug* – down the sink. Then she held her glass up, stuck her nose inside . . . and just sniffed!

As she shuffled out of the kitchen, she handed me the glass of wine. I took a sip of the stuff – it tasted like liquid headache – and then poured the rest into a vase of wilting funeral flowers.

"Remarkable," Ruby-Doo says when he sees the curling stone sitting on my mom's desk like some mammoth paperweight.

"Can I pick it up?"

I nod, and he lifts the stone gently by its curved handle and sits with it in a leather armchair. He rubs his palm over the stone's granite surface, which is bluish grey with these flecks of white.

Till Ruby-Doo, I've told none of my friends about the curling stone: it's sort of moronic having your dad stopped up like a cremated genie in a bottle.

"Tell me about your father," Ruby-Doo says.

So I sit down on my mom's bed and talk about my dad. How he was an English lit prof at CEGEP. How in front of my friends he used expressions like "gee willickers" and "jiminy cricket" just to mortify me.

"Tell me more, Hippie," Ruby-Doo keeps saying. So I keep tripping down memory lane, dodging a few potholes, like how miserable my mom's drinking made my dad.

"His voice," I say, "was a real *twaaangy* drawl 'cause he grew up in *Alabaaama*. And what a motormouth – he was always blabbing away. I'd fade him out like Muzak. But after he died, our house got dead quiet, so I guess I kind of missed the background noise of his voice."

Usually I don't tell people superconfidential things like this. But I do with Ruby-Doo, and I swear he gets all teary-eyed. For a couple seconds, I feel the same awful pain I felt when my dad died – like having shin splints in your heart. But then I glance over at Ruby-Doo and burst out laughing.

"What?" he says. "What's so funny?"

The guy is cradling and petting the curling stone like a frigging pussycat. I take the stone from him and put it back on the desk. Then I pick Ruby-Doo up – he's as light as a girl – and throw him on my mom's bed.

"Hey," he says. "Hey!"

From the living room, my mom yells, "No roughhousing," like we're ten years old.

Ruby-Doo's house is big and dark and crammed with old uncomfortable furniture with claw feet. On the walls are these gloomy sepia photographs of dead relatives.

He's invited me over for his parents' backyard barbecue. I'm expecting hot dogs and hamburgers, but the party is catered. Waiters carrying trays of dinky hors d'oeuvres snake through a crowd of guests. There are men in linen suits and bow ties. There's a woman hired to play violin. Apart from two six-year-old brats who keep winging a Frisbee at the violinist, I'm the youngest person here.

For some privacy, Ruby-Doo and I eat our dessert – sugar pie – on his screened-in veranda. He's jabbering on about this freakazoid named Nicholas Pop, an American artist who transfers genes between species.

"The guy has isolated the green fluorescent protein that makes the Pacific Northwest jellyfish glow," Ruby-Doo says, waving his fork. "And get this: he's injected that gene into the zygote of a guinea pig. Straight into its DNA."

His face lights up and his left knee jiggles as he talks. Watching him, I realize how bizarre my old Saint-Bruno friends would consider Ruby-Doo.

"Under regular light, the animal looks normal – just an albino guinea pig. But add some ultraviolet light and the thing glows an eerie fluorescent green."

"Why call this quack an artist?" I ask. "Is a glow-in-the-dark rodent art?"

"Depends," Ruby-Doo mumbles, his mouth packed with pie. He swallows loudly. "What if art is finding beauty in unexpected places?"

This Pop guy has a Web site: www.chimera.com. Ruby-Doo e-mailed him a sort of fan letter and Pop replied. Seems Pop will be lecturing in Montreal soon and has sent Ruby-Doo two free tickets. Ruby-Doo pulls the tickets from his pocket and hands me one.

"For you, Hippie," he says, patting my knee. "To thank you for listening to my deranged rambling."

The ticket is fluorescent green. On one side is the date of the lecture, along with the address of the theatre. On the other side is one word, which I say out loud: "Glow."

Us eating out, my mom jokes, is how my dad would want his insurance money spent. So every Thursday night, we go to a new restaurant – Indian, Ethiopian, Thai, Mexican, whatever – and try ordering something we don't usually put in our mouths. Tonight, I polish off fava-bean chowder and quail stuffed with apples and thyme; my mom downs escargots with goat cheese and then a bowl of oysters. We're in this homey French place with a dozen tables. Ours is covered in a yellow tablecloth decorated in a pattern of sunflowers and what look like dung beetles.

While I check out the dessert menu, my mom asks how I'm enjoying my summer job.

"I stacked a tub of eggplants today," I say. "Ever notice how beautiful they are? With their little purple bellies like Buddha."

I'm trying to find beauty in unexpected places, but my mother just looks at me funny. "What's happened to my son, the Jock Philistine?" she says.

"The Jock Philistine" is what my old girlfriend, Madison O'Connor, used to call me. Even in front of my mom.

"Heard from Madison lately?" my mom asks, and I shake my head.

Madison wore perfume that smelled like that strawberry powder you mix in milk. After she moved to Chicago, I bought a can of the stuff to remember her by. But by the time I'd finished the can, we'd more or less stopped writing each other.

"Some relationships just fizzle out," my mom says and sighs real dramatically like she's in a play.

"Okay – what's up?"

She plays origami with her napkin a bit. Then blurts out: "Brian proposed to me."

The quail I ate is suddenly pecking its way through my gut.

"I'm going to say no," she says, seeing my stunned look. "We've only been dating four months." She rummages her hands through her hair. "Brian is lovely, but he's . . . a tad boring. I mean, the man's the only anesthesiologist who doesn't need drugs to put a person to sleep."

She laughs at her joke, her trademark guffaw that flashes the fillings in her teeth.

I feel guilty having hassled her about Brian. "You dating," I say, "I think it's a good thing."

My mom raises her eyebrows at me.

"No, I really do," I say and wonder if it's the truth. Then I say what I know is the truth: "Dad would want you to."

I feel sort of bad bringing my father up, but my mom just smiles down at her empty oyster shells, her bowl of castanets.

That night, I overhear my mom talking in her room with the door shut. She says, "One thousand days of sobriety." I assume she's on the phone with one of her batty friends, till she adds, "Can you believe it, Carl?"

She's talking to the curling stone.

On Friday, I have the day off from the grocery store. Around noon, our door buzzer buzzes. When I press the intercom, I hear Ruby-Doo's crackly voice whining, "Can Max come out and play?"

He takes me on a tour of some of his favourite sights in Montreal. Outside Square Victoria metro station, he points out these street lamps: two curvy, lizard-green monstrosities with piss-yellow eyes. They're extraterrestrials attacking a suburban town in a horror flick from the fifties. In a nearby building, we ride his favourite elevator: a birdcage-like contraption operated by a dandruffy old geezer. All the way up, this guy announces the floors in a bilingual garble: "twauziemturdfloor . . . katriemfortfloor."

Later, we walk down a snaky street where cobblestones poke through the asphalt. Sandwiched between two brick triplexes is this tiny wooden house Ruby-Doo wants to show me. It's caramel-coloured and has big shutters and a shingled roof. If we rang the bell, the door would be answered by Hansel and Gretel.

Farther down the street is a little park with a cement statue of a curled-up dog taking a snooze. Ruby-Doo pats the dog's head and says, "What about you, Hippie? What sorts of things do you love?"

Nothing leaps to mind, so I say, "Taking walks with my retarded friend," and Ruby-Doo beams me this sunny smile like I've given him a supreme compliment.

Around suppertime, we wander through the downtown core. The streets are closed off for the jazz festival, and hundreds of people are milling around. A stage is set up in front of the art museum. We find an empty stretch of grass on the museum's lawn and plunk ourselves down. Sitting nearby are two punks: a purple-haired guy and a blue-haired girl, both with shaved eyebrows. Ruby-Doo points out the pet rat Blue Hair has perched on her shoulder. "You think you're special, Hippie," he says. "But dismantle your genome and you'll find you have the same building blocks as that rat."

I'm about to say, *I don't think I'm special*, but stop myself because the day has been one of those perfect days that have you believing you *are* something special.

Ruby-Doo says the rat and I have been put together with the same deluxe set of Lego. "What differs," he says, "is the pieces chosen and the order they're stacked in."

Up on stage, a singer vacuum-packed into a tight dress slinks over to the mike. I lie back in the grass and listen to her low, gravelly voice sing about love and loss and Ruby-Doo's high, cheery voice talk about life and Lego.

We play two-on-one: me against Ruby-Doo and the nurse from *Romeo and Juliet*. The nurse's name is Charlotte, a pretty, twenty-year-old girl who probably didn't get cast as Juliet because she's black and fat.

"Get your skinny butt moving," she yells at Ruby-Doo, lobbing him the ball.

He looks at her in amazement. By the time Charlotte is called back to rehearsal, Ruby-Doo's T-shirt is spotted with sweat like those inkblot tests shrinks use. He falls down on the court. "No more," he huffs. "God have mercy on my skinny white butt."

We head back to my place to eat supper and watch his favourite movie, *2001: A Space Odyssey*. My mom is in the kitchen stirring a wooden spoon in a pot on the stove. "Salut, Max. Salut, Ruby-Doo," she says. "Je vous fais du chili ce soir, les gars."

This bugs me for two reasons. First, only I get to call René-Louis Ruby-Doo. Second, why does my mom always humiliate me with her crappy French?

My mom scoops out some chili and holds the spoon to Ruby-Doo's lips. "Délicieux," he mumbles. Some sauce has smudged on his chin, and my mom wipes it off with a dish towel, slinging an arm across his shoulder. Then she ruffles his hair. My mom has always been touchy-feely, which can be mortifyingly embarrassing.

Ruby-Doo looks at her shyly. "Want to watch the movie with us, Peggy?"

Peggy says she can't because she's leaving in five minutes for AA.

Peggy says AA like it was PTA.

Ruby-Doo looks a bit flustered. "Oh, okay," he says. "Hey, I'm sorry."

"No need to be," my mom insists. "My drinking has been under control for years." Then: "You're surprised because I'm a doctor."

"No, no," he says.

"Some M.D.s even drink on the job," my mom says. "The oath they take is hypocritical rather than Hippocratic." She does her usual guffaw.

As I pour us glasses of water, Ruby-Doo says in his Mr. Science mode that he's read alcoholism is a disease.

More like a self-inflicted wound, I think. My mom once picked me up from Cub Scouts totally plastered. After that, the scout leader always asked how my "home life" was like he was all eager to call Children's Aid.

As my mom natters on, I announce that Ruby-Doo has to take his shower. Once he's gone off to my room, my mom turns to me: "Does my alcoholism still embarrass you?" She jabs her wooden spoon at me. "I've learned to accept it, and so should you."

Sounds like step eight of her twelve-step program.

"Look, what embarrasses me," I say, "is you pawing Ruby-Doo." To be nasty, I add, "Aren't you too old for him?"

She looks straight at me: "You jealous?"

As if I'd be jealous of Ruby-Doo.

After my mom is gone, I peel off my sweaty T-shirt and push open the door to my room. Puddly footprints trail from my bathroom to my dresser. Ruby-Doo stands at the dresser mirror raking a comb across his head. At his feet is his duffel bag with a tumble of clothes hanging out.

I walk up behind him. One of my beach towels circles his waist, and water beads on his back. On the nape of his neck are these little blond hairs.

"So is skinny-ass all clean?" I say. As a joke, I yank his towel off. I'm going to say, *Yep, sure is skinny*, but with him there naked, the words get trapped behind my teeth.

In the mirror, Ruby-Doo is watching me, his pupils the size of pennies. We stare at each other like it's a staring contest, so I feel like the loser when I blink and look away.

He lays his comb down and turns slowly around. I see his blue eye first, then his brown eye. He reaches up, cups a hand around my left biceps.

He squeezes.

I pull away.

"Shower time," I mumble. I hurry into the bathroom, locking the door.

The shower I take is long and cool, but somehow I'm still sweating after I switch off the taps.

During the opening scene, an ape-man swings a club and crushes the skull of a wild boar.

On opposite ends of the couch, Ruby-Doo and I sit watching 2001. His voice cracking like a thirteen-year-old puberty case, Ruby-Doo says, "It's good your mom goes to AA."

I say, "Uh-huh." I keep my eyes glued to the TV screen and spoon chili into my mouth.

In another scene, a spacecraft flies to the moon. On board is a stewardess who wears shoes with Velcro soles to anchor her to the floor.

Later, when Ruby-Doo finally leaves, I walk around our apartment like that stewardess. Taking careful, measured steps so I don't float off into zero gravity.

For the next few days, Ruby-Doo is in Quebec City attending his older sister's wedding. I stack Swiss chard and bok choy; I stack tangerines and mangoes.

I call up Pete, an old friend from Saint-Bruno, and we go skating on the bike paths that criss-cross the Plateau. Pete is tall and gangly; he has red hair and a smattering of freckles. With rollerblades on, he's a giraffe on wheels.

We buy hot dogs blanketed in sauerkraut and wolf them down sitting on a stoop outside a french-fry place. Pete nudges me and nods toward two girls sitting nearby. He whispers, "Eager beavers," his expression for girls on the make.

I look over at the girls. Then I look past them, down a back lane where every duplex has an outdoor spiral staircase twisting from the ground to the top balcony.

During our walking tour, Ruby-Doo compared Montreal's spiral staircases to DNA.

I wonder what he's doing at this exact moment. What he's thinking about. Then I realize it's damn faggy to wonder these things and that I'd better snap out of it.

So I go talk to the girls with Pete. I make jokes. I flash a big cheesy smile. To show off, I do a handstand with my skates on. With my T-shirt riding up, the blood pooling in my head, the hot dog somersaulting in my stomach, I almost feel normal.

Last year, I'm at this party thrown by this guy Charlie Deller, a basketball player from another school. At one point, Charlie takes me into his dad's study. At the wet bar, he pours us glasses of crème de menthe, which tastes like concentrated mouthwash. Charlie is a little drunk. One minute he's bragging about bench-pressing one-eighty; next minute he leans over and licks my cheek like it's a frigging ice-cream cone. "You've got nice skin," he says, just before his girlfriend walks in.

A week later, our b-ball team plays his. Charlie Deller sees me, says, "Hey man, how's it going?" All nonchalant like it isn't queer for people to go around licking faces.

Charlie decides to ignore what happened. Pretty smart move because now whenever I bump into him, I practically think I dreamed the whole cheek-licking episode up.

Saturday afternoon, I'm in the park, slam-dunking a few when Ruby-Doo rides up on his clunky bicycle, a knapsack strapped to his back. I go over to say hi, hugging the b-ball to my stomach; I ask how the wedding was.

"Stuffy. Overblown," he says. "It made me want to live in sin."

Ruby-Doo smiles, and I feel creepy, like maybe he's implying *we* should live in sin. So I look down at a little sandy anthill spilling out of a crack in the concrete. I smudge the anthill with my foot.

Ruby-Doo opens the drawstring of his knapsack and yanks out a big box wrapped in aluminum foil. "For you," he says, handing it over.

I stand there staring at the box, my throat as dry as a tortilla chip.

"Well, go ahead and open it." He rubs his palms on his jeans like he's wiping away sweat.

I unpeel the foil. It's a shoebox. Inside are Riko basketball sneakers. Fire-hydrant-red stripes and air-bubble soles. Tongues sticking out at me.

"It's not my birthday."

"So what," Ruby-Doo says. "Try them on. You take nine and a half, right?"

I sit on the bench, wriggle my old sneakers off, and lace the Rikos up. Then I boing up and down the court, thinking, *So he bought you a gift. Means nothing.*

"Perfect fit," I say.

"Look at you," Ruby-Doo shouts with a big smile. "Cinderella of the basketball court."

I glare at him: "What'd you call me?"

"What?" he says.

In the pissed-off yell-whisper my mom uses on me, I snap, "I'm no Cinderella, okay."

"Okay, okay," Ruby-Doo replies. Then a sly look flits across his face. "But you got to admit," he says, "when it comes to princes, I'm pretty charming."

My anger stings like a rug burn.

I rip the left Riko off and throw it on the ground. The right Riko I whip across the court at Ruby-Doo's head, smacking him hard in the face.

He flinches. Cups a hand over his nose.

I just stand there, embarrassed. Like a ten-year-old who's had a tantrum in public.

Ruby-Doo draws his hand away. I expect blood, but there's none. Still, his nose is blotchy and his eyes are red and teary.

He walks toward me.

I look down at my stocking feet; I expect him to punch me and I hope he does. But he brushes past, his shoulder skimming mine. Under his breath, he mutters, "You're welcome."

When I get home, I shove the Rikos under my bed with my old puzzles and dinosaur models and sports trophies.

Nauseous and dizzy – that's how I feel. Like my organs – heart, stomach, pituitary gland – are strapped into a Rotowhirl at the midway.

I lie on my bed.

I try to think. I try to stay calm. I try to be logical.

Okay, proof I'm not queer: I did it with Madison once. So what if it wasn't that romantic. We had a bath together first and she'd poured in tons of bubble-bath powder. Well, the stuff left a gross soapy film on our skin. Still, all my parts worked the way they're supposed to. The whole time I kept thinking we were performing some weird calisthenics for gym class.

I think, *Do I want to do calisthenics with Ruby-Doo?*

Then I feel totally disgusted. At myself for hurting Ruby-Doo. At Ruby-Doo for calling me his princess.

And especially at myself for wanting to hold Ruby-Doo after I hurt him.

Later there's a knock on my bedroom door.

"Go away!" I yell at my mom.

She comes in anyway, spritzing her neck with eau de toilette and wearing a blouse that looks like the stuff they make doilies out of. She flushed Brian last week and already has a coffee date with some chatroom conquest she met on the Internet.

"How do I look?"

I lie that she has too much lipstick on, and she kisses a Kleenex to blot her mouth.

"I hope you know," I say, "that women are entrapped on the Net and sold into white slavery."

Picking invisible lint from her skirt, she says, "Sometimes, Max, you've got to be willing to take such chances."

I want to say, *Don't go.* Not that I'm afraid her date is an axe murderer. Or that I don't want her meeting someone, getting over my father. Or even that I want to talk about what's eating me. I'd just like her here, that's all. Putzing around the apartment the way moms do, while I sulk in my room.

She bends down, kisses my forehead. "You still going out with René-Louis tonight?" she asks.

I shrug. That lecture with the damn glow-in-the-dark rodent is at 7:00. My green fluorescent ticket is thumbtacked to my bulletin board.

After my mom leaves, I pour myself some Cheerios for supper. But my appetite is shot, so I leave the little life preservers floating in their milk.

I pace around the apartment. Drift from room to room. I end up in my mom's room, flipping through *Romeo and Juliet*, which I spot on her bookshelf. It's my dad's classroom copy, all dog-eared and mangled. In the margins, he's pencilled in his comments.

"Love isn't a play on words," he's written in Act II. "Rather it's words at play, let out at recess to go swing on the monkey bars."

What the fuck does that mean?

Suddenly I'm furious with my dad for being so frigging cryptic, for not being here to set me straight. For being stone-cold dead.

I grab up the curling stone and go into our bowling-alley hallway. I slide that sucker down the hall with such force it smacks against the back wall, nicking the paint and leaving a monster dent.

I sit on the floor.

I jab the tips of my index fingers into the corners of my eyes to stop myself from bawling.

It doesn't work.

Once, when I was thirteen, I saw my dad cry.

We were staying at our cottage on Danforth Lake. I'd been off picking raspberries. When I got back, I could hear my mom's voice: loud and gin-and-tonicky. She was on the patio with the German couple from the cottage next door.

When she saw me, she screeched, "There's my baby!"

To get away from her, I went down to the dock. My dad was sitting there, his feet dangling in the water. I snuck up, hoping to scare him. But before I could yell "Raahh!" the dock creaked and my dad turned his head.

His cheeks were wet, his eyes bloodshot. Snot was rolling out of his nose.

I was terrified.

Still, I sat down beside him, dunked my feet in the water, and watched tadpoles as big as kiwi fruit nibble at my toes.

"You hate her, don't you?" I finally said. "You hate her guts."

"No, Max," he said, wiping the snot with the back of his hand. "I was crying because I love her guts."

It's 7:30 by the time I reach Ex-Centris, the theatre where Nicholas Pop is giving his talk on glowing rodents. Out front, a dozen picketers are traipsing up and down the sidewalk. They wear green glow-in-the-dark necklaces and wave placards: BRILLER, C'EST PAS BRILLANT! and REMEMBER DR. FRANKENSTEIN!

The beefy guy at the door doesn't want to let me in, but when I whip out my ticket, he sweeps me through. Ex-Centris is one long lobby with a stone floor and a glass ceiling. Off the lobby are three rooms. The ticket girl says I'm late and points me toward the Salle Fellini.

I slink inside this low-lit hall where a guy dressed in black is on stage talking. Scanning the audience – there must be two hundred people here – I finally spot the back of Ruby-Doo's head near the front.

As I'm wedging into the second row, the guy on stage – Pop, I guess – says, "I don't care about aesthetics. Aesthetics to me is what primatology is to monkeys." The audience starts laughing; so does Ruby-Doo, till he sees me toddling toward him. After stepping my Rikos on seventeen feet, I shoehorn myself into the empty seat beside him.

"Hi," I whisper.

"Well, if it ain't Cinderella's ugly stepsister," he mutters, looking straight ahead.

"Yeah," I say.

There's a chalky taste, like a dissolved Aspirin, in my mouth. I turn and face the stage. That's when I notice the albino guinea pig. It's inside a see-through plastic hutch set on a table near Pop.

"Man has tinkered with the evolution of plants and animals for thousands of years. So creating hybrids violates no social precedence," Pop says, his voice booming through some hidden mike. The guy is a preacher with a rock star's goatee and leather pants. He talks on about jellyfish and mutation and enzymes while a screen behind him flashes images of Petri dishes, X and Y chromosomes, and whatnot.

I'm barely paying attention. Instead I listen to Ruby-Doo's breath going in and out. *Here's what you do*, I think. *Apologize. Tell him he's a great guy, a good friend – but just a friend. Then do a Charlie Deller and pretend nothing happened.*

Pop fishes his guinea pig out of its cage. Its hind legs pirouette as the guy tucks the animal to his chest. We're seated so close I can see the guinea pig's dark red eyes, which look like beads of blood.

"My aim with little Chimera," Pop says, petting the animal's white fur and pink petal ears, "is to challenge what we define as genetically pure. What we define as otherness."

The guinea pig squirms in Pop's arms, squeaking like a baby's squeeze toy.

"Green fluorescent protein," Pop says, "doesn't change the creature in any significant way but one."

Just then, angry shouts erupt in the lobby.

Pop's booming voice says, "But what tremendous importance we place on that one thing."

The theatre's back doors bang open, and we all swivel in our seats. The picketers march through, chanting, "Hell, no, we won't glow!" One protester tosses leaflets in the air. A woman in an aisle seat jumps up and tries wrestling away a placard, but she stumbles backward with a yelp into some guy's lap. Meanwhile, the beefy doorman storms in red-faced and growling, "Câlice de tabarnac!"

Ruby-Doo turns toward me, his left leg brushing against my right . . . and I swear I want to move away but my leg stays put.

"Bedlam," he says with a grin.

"Totally," I whisper.

Up on stage, Pop nods toward the projection room. Off go all the house lights. For two seconds, pitch blackness. Then a loud click. Then a bluish shaft of light beaming down from the rafters.

In Pop's arms, the white guinea pig turns a brilliant green. Like crème de menthe. Like a traffic light telling you to go. Like the glowing skin of Frankenstein's monster.

It's very weird and really scary.

And kind of beautiful in an unexpected way.

JOCELYN BROWN

Miss Canada

Marjorie wants to be contestant number four but she can't be because I am. I know all the rules so I'm the referee and the referee goes last. Rita's before me and Lorraine's before Rita, so move it Marjorie, I say, or you'll be disqualified. You have three seconds. We don't have all day, shouts Berte from the living room, pigface Berte who gets her own room and gets to be a judge because she's too spazzy to play. Rita goes shut your face Berte but I say okay okay, and push Marjorie. Marjorie grabs the towel rack with both hands and yells, hey Mom I'm going last. We have to do the skin-twister on her, me on one arm, Lorraine on the other – Marjorie bites Lorraine's arm, Lorraine kicks her, we push her out of the bathroom (the change area, Rita calls it), slam the door. I make the announcement: the talent section has begun. Marjorie always dances, puts her rain boots on and pretends to be a go-go dancer from *Go-Go 66*. She bashes into the plant stand in the hallway so the orange plant pot Aunt Sherrie made at ceramics class breaks and there's dirt all over the place. Oh god what now says Mom from the living room, with her hands covering her face probably, and it wasn't my fault, goes Marjorie at the same time. Zero talent marks for Miss Petit Dejeuner, I say.

You're not the judge, screeches Marjorie, you're not the judge of me. Shut up we all yell back, shut up or we'll have to quit. Just go, says Rita, just go Marjorie, I'll put on your record. Rita slides into the living room and Berte screams those are my socks Rita, take them off you bitch, take them off. Berte tries to grab Rita. That's what she does, grabs your wrist with one hand, scratches your arm with the other – we all have little scars. After that time Rita punched her and Berte fell and cut her head on the corner of the coffee table and they had to take another trip to emergency, Mom said we're not allowed to hit Berte back. Berte's still going, take them off, take them off, bitch bitch fucking bitch. Mom yells quiet, Rita says I hate you Berte, I hope you die, and puts on "These Boots are Made for Walking."

We watch Marjorie from the doorway, Rita and me and Lorraine, barely poking our heads in because watching other contestants is against the rules now. Mom's feet are the only part of Mom we can see, her feet rubbing each other. Marjorie, she goes in a big sigh like someone pulled out a plug, Marjorie please stay on the floor. No fair, that's not fair, Frances stood on the table to sing once, no fair, goes Marjorie. Her voice gets louder, squeakier, until we're all yelling stop, Marjorie stop. Mom goes fine, sigh, just move the coffee table away from the TV. We hold our ears as it scrapes across the floor and Mom curls her toes under like Aunt Paula used to when she got seizures, Aunt Paula whose false teeth flew into Lorraine's ice cream that time. Rita starts the record again and with arms and hair all over the place Marjorie shouts, let's welcome Contestant Number One, Miss Petit Dejeuner, the talented dancer, yaaay. She claps like a moron and we see her panties as she climbs onto the table and then we just wait for her to fall off which she always does. Marjorie's feet thump up and down like the table's burning hot and she slugs her own head with her own flying arm and doesn't even look surprised, just keeps that retard smile. Then both feet thump down at the same time, both too close to the edge. Rita squeezes my shoulders hard and we wait for the crash and the screams and the oh-god-what-now sigh. Mom and Rita go to help but Marjorie pushes them away, screaming stop laughing, even though they're not, not even smiling. Mom says, thank you Miss Petit Dejeuner, that was lovely, and Frances, she says to me, there are no marks taken off for falling. Marjorie goes to the kitchen, slams cupboard doors, and stay out of the crackers, says Mom. Don't touch my pop Lorraine yells. She gets Mountain Dew with her allowance and saves it for Walt Disney.

Rita and me always spend our allowance right away but Rita gets more money from Dad's pockets while he's sleeping. I'm looking for Mom's bathing suit, she says if he wakes up. Rita buys me chips and twice she took me to *The Sound of Music* on Saturdays instead of the library like Mom thought. People look at Rita and smile, and the ones who know her say I can't believe that kid's only ten. Before we play, when we're all in the kitchen, Mom pulls on Rita's T-shirt, looks down and goes we'll have to ask Dad for money to get you a brassiere, I wonder where he is. Rita drops a plate, not on purpose, and fat pig Berte says yeah really after Mom says, thank god it wasn't a good one. Rita goes downstairs and Lorraine says let's play Miss Canada. Mom strains the potatoes, her face all steamy, her glasses barely hanging on to the end of her nose and says okay. Okay, but just until Dad gets home and we can have supper. When I go to get Rita, Mom remembers Dad keeps his magazines and stuff in the basement and yells, you two get out of there. Rita clunks the dryer door and yells back we're getting our costumes, but we what we really do is shake every can of Berte's Craigmont ginger ale. Berte has a whole box of her own pop we're not allowed to touch.

Lorraine is Miss Miracle Whip and she waits in the hall like a block of cement. She always wins the talent portion because she's the only one who takes Highland Dancing so she's the only one who can do a sword dance. With closed eyes and silent moving lips, she touches the perfect pleats in her kilt. You're not allowed to do the same thing more than twice, I say, you did the sword dance the last two times, you'll be disqualified. But she knows Mom's always on her side and doesn't even open her eyes. Lorraine gets her own bed, which should be Rita's because Rita is second oldest after Berte who gets a whole room to herself. Rita said, big hairy deal, Uncle George died on that bed anyways, but it's still not fair. Every night Mom lays on Lorraine's bed when she comes upstairs, lays down every night and says Lorraine has such beautiful skin, Lorraine makes such a good pillow, Lorraine is so so soft. Rita and me and Marjorie are squished in the other bed, Marjorie trying to hog all the blankets, Rita grinding her teeth like she's chewing raw spaghetti.

What Lorraine also has is a shoebox of beads, a box full of her own tiny beads under her own bed and the last thing I hear every night is her hand swirling through them.

Finally Mom and Berte hold up Marjorie's marks. We're allowed to look but not to say anything, except for me if I have to say a rule was broken. Berte's paper has a messy 2.5 on it, and Berte looks at Mom with a little I'm-so-wonderful smile. Mom holds up 5.0. That's way too high, some for effort, okay, but poise and talent count for more and no way Marjorie gets anything for that. No way she gets 5.0 for falling off a table. The referee disagrees, I say, there must be at least two full points deducted for a fall. Frances, says Mom, shut up. She can't get more than four point zero, I say, that's the rule, but Mom goes, Christ, and lays down. Mom has never said shut up to me before, only to Rita, and then she goes who-do-you-think-you-are-for-God's-sake-shut-up-this-minute, never just shut up. I look for Rita but she's smoking one of Dad's butts in the change area. Rita and me always do a duet for the talent portion. We made a deal after the first Miss Canada, after the first winning sword dance which was two points higher than me singing "House of the Rising Sun" and three points higher than Rita reciting "Only God Can Make a Tree." I promised not to sing again because Rita can't, and Lorraine would beat me anyways. Rita and I promised each other we'd play duets for talent, "Country Gardens" or the first page of "Finlandia" which was all we had time to learn before Mrs. Bentley's daughter went on a Mormon mission to Iowa and stopped teaching us. If there are no mistakes we get 4.5, which is all we would get on our own anyways, and Rita can try to win the evening gown and swimsuit competitions, and I'm good at the skill-testing question and congeniality. It's so unfair that Lorraine can do the same thing over and over – that's all she knows how to do and it's enough to win. Her stupid kilt goes back and forth and she touches the swords, which is a mistake but she knows it doesn't matter. Mom is clapping anyways.

Rita leans against the doorway and I lean against her knees, hoping she'll play with my hair like sometimes she does. Instead she wipes her nose on a sock. She throws the sock into the living room. Berte screams pick it up, pick it up, pick it up and

Lorraine's foot lands right on the sword. Lorraine falls and cries, Mom that doesn't count. Oh yes it does, I say, oh yes it does. Falls always count, two points off. Berte's still screaming, so is Lorraine, and Rita stands so Berte can see her, spits on the other sock, drops it. Berte tries to run for Rita but falls over the sword and Rita goes ha ha I hope you die. Mom doesn't know what's going on, she didn't see the socks. Mom says, Berte did you take your medicine today, for God's sake calm down. She looks at Rita and says, wipe that smirk off your face. Rita keeps smiling and Mom says, that kid is so disturbed. Lorraine drags Berte off the sword, makes it into a cross again, turns the music way up and dances, does her dumb little kicks with pointy toes. Berte gets up, falls, slaps away Mom who tries to help, gets up again and goes for her socks. Marjorie's back from the basement, burps a huge gross ginger-ale burp and laughs her machine-gun laugh while Rita digs tiny holes in the doorway trim with a nailfile. Berte thinks they're laughing at her and goes for Rita, falls against Marjorie who cuts her ankle on a piece of ceramic from Aunt Sherrie's plant pot. Berte gets Marjorie's wrist and starts scratching, Rita puts her arm around Berte's neck and chokes her so Berte lets go of Marjorie who's bleeding. Knock it off, yells Mom, knock it off right now or that's it. I get Berte back to the chesterfield with her socks, Rita puts her hand over Marjorie's mouth and promises her a quarter if she'll be quiet. Lorraine finally finishes dancing. Mom claps.

Berte's crying Rita choked me, and Mom sees this teeny red mark on Berte's neck and says, this is the final straw Rita, the final straw. I touch the back of Rita's hair, pull the flippy part straight, and say I don't want to do a duet this time. She's holding a wet cold tea towel over Marjorie's cut. I'm going on my own, I say, it's easier. Rita turns and looks at me. I see her inside her eyes and her eyes inside her and on and on like the Pot of Gold lady holding chocolates that have a picture of her holding chocolates on it, and a picture inside that picture and on and on until you can barely see her. In the tiniest Rita I can see, I know she has to win. I'm going to sing, I say.

Rita can't sing, can't carry a tune to save her life, says Mom. When everyone else sings Christmas carols or "Happy Birthday,"

Rita mouths the words, and sometimes she does it to records too, with her eyes closed, dancing, sort of. I'll give you 50¢ if you don't sing she tells me. I'll let you wear my hairbands. I'll let you use my new eyeshadow. I say no. Can I wear your hairbands, Rita, goes Marjorie, her nose all runny. Rita says no.

Lorraine's mark comes right away, 5.8 as usual. I count to twenty and say, Miss Miracle Whip is disqualified, she didn't introduce the next competitor, it has to be within twelve seconds of the bow, that's the rule. Mom's toes are all crossed and her feet curl up again. No way goes Lorraine, Marjorie didn't for me. Marjorie doesn't count I say. But of course Mom sticks up for Lorraine and says, Miss Miracle Whip just do it now, please. So Lorraine looks all bored like she's giving a social report or something and says, the next contestant is Miss Velveeta. Rita doesn't move. She's supposed to go within ten seconds of being announced, and Berte counts backwards all excited like it's New Year's, three two one zero, then yells Miss Velveeta is disqualified. Rita stays still and Berte goes, she's so mental, to Mom who says to me, move it Miss Cherry Blossom, let's get this over with. I squish by Rita and Mom's eyes are closed and she's completely lying down. I stand on a clean spot of linoleum and think of soldiers waiting in the kitchen for me, my whole country listening, and a big movie camera close to my face. Very soft, very slow, I start "Edelweiss" like I'm nervous, but I'm not, not at all. Mom opens her eyes but I don't look at her, I look far away, through the pink wall that was supposed to be melon except the man at the paint store made a mistake. Then, just like in the movie, "Edelweiss" gets louder and stronger, it comes all the way from my toes, from all of me, and I know I'm going to win. Even if I lose the swimsuit competition and I don't get Miss Congeniality, I know this time I'll be Miss Canada.

MIKE BARNES

Cogagwee

(Walks Around the Life of Tom Longboat)

I ran. No one could catch me. Only a few could beat me.

There was a glass jar inside my window, between the glass and the torn screen. It had six sides and no lid. A long black bug flew into the jar and did not fly out. (Could not? Would not? I wonder now. But not then.) I watched it walk across the bottom of the jar and try to walk up the smooth sides. But it slipped off them, sliding or falling down. It tried again, on one side or another. Three or four other beetles – dead, dried husks – littered the bottom of the jar. The walking beetle stepped over and around them.

Mother came into the room while I was watching the walking beetle. Briskly, she upended the jar on the sill and slapped at the contents with a newspaper. Once, twice. Her face alert and irritated throughout. "Don't watch a trapped thing die," she snapped. "Kill it or let it go." She flicked the scraps up onto the newspaper, balled it.

She left the room. I stared at the empty jar, its movement erased. But still somehow present. It hadn't occurred to me that the insect was dying. But the idea did not seem surprising or important. I had been watching it walk with its six legs.

∼

"Catch me if you can," Mother said. I never did.

The Globe, Boxing Day, 1906: LONGBOAT ALWAYS WINS
 And that year, my nineteenth on earth, for a few months, I did. Wins:

   Victoria Day, Caledonia. Took lead over five miles and never lost it.

   "Around the Bay," Hamilton. Caught John Marsh napping on the Stone Road and opened up three minutes on him before the tape. At the awards ceremony outside the *Hamilton Herald*, Bill Sherring predicted, You won't win pretty but you'll win.

   Ward Marathon, Toronto. Fifteen miles. High Park west along Lakeshore Road, and back again. Burned out Bill Cumming (and seventy-two others). Won by three minutes.

   Christmas Day, Hamilton. Cumming and I duelled on icy, hard-rutted road. Halfway along, about the five-mile mark, a rig trotting beside us skidded on the ice and fell over on us. We squeezed out from under and kept going. My 54:50 broke the old course record by more than two minutes.

First year: 0 for 1. Second: 4 for 4. My perfect season.

"Interesting a study as the world's champion long distance runner makes – as Indian first and before all – with, over those deep racial attributes, the light veneer of the white man's ways and habits, of far deeper interest is the girl he is about to wed. Here the Indian traits are well covered. . . . Few would imagine that she had been born and raised on an Indian reservation and was of Indian blood. In every way she is a winsome little girl who has, as she says, been educated away from many of the traditions of her race. She does not like to talk of feathers,

war paint or other Indian paraphernalia. She is ambitious
for Tom and if anybody can make a reliable man and good citizen
of that elusive being, Thomas Longboat, it will be his wife."

Lauretta read it out like a teacher at the Institute, enunciat-
ing primly, shoulders back, hand on hip. She cracks me up. I was
laughing out loud by the end, and she must've wanted to, but she
kept her poker face.

"Lord-a-miracle," I said, "how'd you like to get scalped?"

"Is that what we're calling it now?" she said. Still prissy-like.

"Watch out for the tomahawk!"

Her smoky smell gets stronger when she sweats. We were
lying side by side. Red lips over her ribs where I'd pinched her,
hard, made her giggle finally.

"What's 'elusive being'?"

She answered after a bit. "It means no one can catch you."

"Pietri couldn't anyway," I said.

We were silent for a bit. Sounds of the hotel, and streets
below. New York. My mind went ahead four days, to the
rematch with Pietri. He would want it.

"And 'winsome'?"

"Happy, I guess. Cheerful."

"Are you?"

"Cheerful?"

I shoved her. "Happy."

"Sure. Sometimes."

"Now?"

"Sure."

Martha Silversmith was a good wife too, though she lacked
Lauretta's mischief and her rebel fun. Then again, Lauretta was
younger, and perhaps Martha had more to contend with. All
Lauretta had to face was me getting killed and then coming
back to life again.

(Spring morning. A robin bulgy with eggs on a stump outside
the window, orange on brown on blue. Lauretta's new husband

rattling cups and dishes in the kitchen, letting us know he's there. "Tom, I'm awful glad you're alive," Lauretta says, "but I think I'll stay where I am." That twitch at the corner of her mouth which you never knew if she meant or not.

We were sitting at her kitchen table in Ohsweken.

When the robin flew up and my eyes followed it, I saw a raccoon curled up on the corner of the neighbour's second-floor porch, dozing in the sun. Chew marks on the lattice told me the work he was resting from. When Lauretta went to reassure the rattler, I rapped on the glass. The way the coon sat up and sniffed, plus the awkward splay of his fat rear, gave me an idea, and when Lauretta returned, I said, "I wasn't dead. Just hibernating."

"I don't need a bear any more than I need a ghost." Quick, Lauretta, so quick.)

Martha Silversmith. Lauretta Maracle. I only married women with beautiful names.

Sometimes it seemed Martha and I were running, sprinting full bore after something, and sometimes it seemed we were standing still. Hardly ever walking, though I tried to find that pace. Running and standing still are much closer to each other than either is to walking. I saw the plum side of that when I won the marathon in Boston. After I caught Petch on the Newton Hills, I felt like I was standing still. Policemen pushing people back at the end and I could see every face clearly, Rockefeller on a riverboat, watching the faces on the banks float past. Hands brushing me like branches, but still separated from them. By water, by current.

Afterwards, a terrific steak dinner. Then the governor of Massachusetts presents me with a gold medal (for breaking the record) and a bronze statue of Mercury. As I'm hoisting it up before the cheering crowd, suddenly I feel air fanning my face, cheers and shouts lost in a wind roar, and I glance up and see the wings on Mercury's bronze feet spinning to a blur, like hummingbird wings. The faces too all just blurs, smudges lost to speed.

~

When your father dies and you are only five, many people assume you spend your whole life looking for a mentor. Untrue. Advice is overrated; you have to learn everything yourself. Every mistake must be made at least once. And when you do find yourself needing a guide, a teacher, there will generally be one close at hand. Overall, I had more trouble shucking off mentors than I did finding them. I have no memories of my father.

~

Running children.

When I was twelve and finished grade four in the band school, they enrolled me in the Mohawk Institute, the Anglican mission boarding school in Brantford. Two rules: no "long-house practices" (which would have made Mother laugh; she always said that longhouse was just the Bible watered down for Indians – "They know the hard stuff goes to our heads" – and that Handsome Lake should've been paid by the missionaries and maybe he was). No "Indian," only English. That was a bigger problem.

The hours I spent standing in the corner at the back of the classroom. Glancing up I could see a painting of Joseph Brant and the poster of Pauline Johnson, which might have been hung there for my benefit. She wore a bear-claw necklace and fringed and beaded buckskin.

Tekahionwake
(Miss E. Pauline Johnson,
The Iroquois Indian Poet-Entertainer)

She was a handsome woman (Lauretta resembled her, though softer-faced and plumper), and the Institute's most famous student. "If you mock her, you mock all of us," intoned the fat, laced-up teacher in a dangerously soft voice. It was Art period and she was standing behind me. I stared down at my paper (which in a few seconds she would tear to pieces) –

myself in shorts, raising my lacrosse stick after a goal
Cogagwee
(Mr. Thomas Longboat
The Onondagan Lacrosse Champion)

– wondering if something my pencil and a dreaming mood had traced could really have such a sharp point.

No running (except in P.E. class). No fishing.

The first time I left, I was weeding the Institute garden. Cabbage whites flitted about my head. Bent over in a row between peas and carrots, watching green coil and feather upwards in the sun, feeling myself sink down the other way, muscles pooling like butter. A black bug walked a lime stalk: nothing. The last thought I had before I started running was, *I might as well be weeding Mother's garden* (which would have handed her another laugh).

They caught me, punished me. But the next time, I made it all the way to my uncle's, who said he'd hide me if I worked for him.

All the way up the road swinging an imaginary lacrosse stick, snaring passes from blurred wingers on one side, snapping them into blurred nets on the other, stampstampstamp, brain hollering *CogagweeCogagweeCogagwee – EverythingEverything-Everything* – as all the Indian and English names drop behind me in the dust.

Later the Institute would ask me back, but I declined all requests to appear. The first invitation came after I won the Boston; they came periodically after that, and frequently after Pauline Johnson died in 1913, just before the war. They needed another example. So did I.

Arguments with both wives on this score. Lauretta could recite "The Song My Paddle Sings" by heart; so could Martha (hell, *I* knew most of it), but with her it was more a matter of don't refuse an invitation: it's unlucky and who knows when you'll get another. A good woman, but fearful.

"I left the Institute," was all I ever said. Many times. To both of them.

1930. Thirty years almost to the day that I ran from the Institute, I made a guest appearance at the Canadian National Exhibition. I smiled at the spectators, started a race. Afterwards, my eight-year-old daughter ran across the street to greet me and was killed by a car. Her body flew through the air a short way, then fell to the ground with a thud. Like a shot goose, not much bigger.

Later, holding Martha as she cried and blamed me. "You can't stop a child from running," I said, and was sorry I said.

But can you? And would you if you could?

Martha's shoulders shaking as she sobbed, my mind running. *Would I? Would I? Would I?*

Globe and Mail, 1937.

Youngsters in North Toronto are fired with a new ambition, not merely to be engine drivers, G-men or even cowboys. Their growing ambition now is to be a street cleaner. That is what their idol is – a man who 30 years ago was the most famous athlete in the world and the idol of Canada. . . . "Oh, I'm not news any more," protested the once famous marathoner when a reporter discovered him sweeping leaves on Lawrence Avenue today. "I've had my day – and no regrets."

"You're a pretty important fellow to the children of this district," answered the reporter.

"Well, I'm glad they like me," smiled the big Onondaga Indian. "Maybe all I'm good for now is sweeping leaves, but if I can help the kids and show them how to be good runners and how to lead a clean life, I'm satisfied."

Note: I was never "big." Was five foot nine, maybe 145 pounds by then (I ran at 132).

Evening Walks (I).

From 1919 to 1926, I mostly kept to a comfortable stroll. Others might have worried (Martha did!), but I felt I knew the pace and the road.

Went out west to see if I could scare up a veteran's homestead grant, but no luck. Saw a lot of pretty country though, moving from town to town. All manner of jobs: digging ditches, mucking barns, baling hay.

Then back to Ontario, since Martha wanted to raise the kids closer to Ohsweken. Worked Dunlop Rubber in Toronto, then the Steel Company in Hamilton.

"Doc" was a janitor at the Steel Company. His nickname came from the rumour that he had been a doctor before and during the Great War, but had returned to work as a labourer. Others found him strange, but I found him to be a true gentleman, courteous and soft-spoken. We'd already been working together three months when Doc showed me a scrapbook he'd kept of my exploits before the war. The curious (and slightly embarrassing) part was that Doc had cut and pasted headlines, pictures, and articles not just about my running but also about my marriages, my children's births, the scandals about my "professional" status, my enlistment (and death) in the army. Mostly from the Toronto papers, but Doc even had the sideview shot of my naked lower half (privates artfully concealed) – "Tom Longboat's $20,000 Legs" – published in the *New York Telegram*.

Flipping through Doc's scrapbook was like flipping through my life. Reliving it in shutter clicks.

The last article was only a month old. From the title, "Walking Into the Sunset," I got the gist and knew it was a cornball piece. My eyes skipped down and found the phrase "falling from the limelight into obscurity." I guess nobody'd told the reporter everyone does that.

"I've had a good run," I mumbled, closing the book.

And now Doc – who normally you had to crowbar words out of – told me that he and I had the same birthday. Same day, same year. That shook me more than his scrapbook had. I stared hard at him a few moments. He looked at least ten years older than me. Broom-bent, veiny-bald, his eyes starting to film. But then I've kept in shape, never stopped walking.

It was about six months later that I got my layoff slip. Production was slowing down. Doc was safe, of course – he had eight years in, and a janitor is always needed – but he seemed to take it hardest of all. I was emptying my locker after a long shower, the rest of the gang already cleared out, when I heard a gulp behind me. Doc was sitting hunched over at the other end of the bench, crying almost silently. One hand over his eyes, his shoulders shaking. Hardly any sound. I didn't know what to do other than move down closer to him. I was standing behind him, my hand floating towards his shoulder, when Doc blurted, "I saw you run in England."

I pulled my hand back. This little man kept surprising me. It was certainly possible. I ran races with the 180th Sportsmen's Battalion in England, then with the 3rd Reserve, still in England. Races, too, in France, at first. With the 107th then, the "Red" (or "Injin") Battalion. February. June, I think. August, near Vimy. I didn't know anything about Doc's life.

"I *saw* you run." Quieter and fiercer now. His wet eyes glaring, his hands white-knuckled on the mop handle. If there ever was a picture of a man running *and* standing still, it was Doc just then. Which told me what to do.

I leaned the mop against the wall and led him by the elbow out into the wide clanking night. We walked around the Steel Company premises, among and between all the hulking black shapes. Men in sooty shadows, smoking or hiding. It was a pleasant cool night, the air decent and fresh, thanks to a west wind blowing the bad smells east. Doc kept peering upwards, but the yard lights and flames killed the stars. I walked him along the coke oven tracks and we saw a "push" just ahead of us. Red glowing coke tumbling out of the oven into a waiting rail car, orange sparks flurrying upward. Better than fireworks because it meant something. Further on, where the track ended, we had a good view of the dark bay with two freighters, black oblongs, moored in it. There were two huge hills, dark silhouettes, humped up to points, with soft sides rounding down. This was the iron ore and coal the ships had left behind. Right between the two peaks was a little curl of moon, bright white.

"Egypt," Doc said, his voice almost a whisper. The piles did look like pyramids, their edges gentled by centuries.

That's the way, I thought, and I clapped him between the shoulder blades in encouragement. That's when I felt it. A tingle, small but unmistakable, like a current passing through my fingertips into Doc's back. Mother's words came tumbling back to me: "Spirit's just like food or money. You can earn it, spend it, lose it, hoard it, give it away." She recommended the first and the last as the best courses, and I knew I'd just followed her advice and passed on a little soul bread to someone who needed it more.

Hibernation (or: My Activities While Deceased).

It was like the end of a long, lost marathon. Like the end of my Olympic dream, 1908, in London, when, running a strong second, almost without warning, my legs turned to slush and I dropped. False accusations later that Flanagan, my manager, had drugged me (after running up the odds in my favour, then counter-betting). Flanny only gave me a stimulant when I was already twitching on the ground, bleeding from my nose and mouth. No, something poisonous was in the air that day. Something that took men out of the race. Hefferon's lead died – he finished, but they carried him off in a stretcher. Pietri staggered into the stadium, turned the wrong way round, collapsed, was helped up, staggered, collapsed, fell again, got up . . . there was a film of all this, and I could hardly believe it when I watched. Finally, Pietri fell and didn't move. Hayes entered the stadium. That's when the officials panicked, I guess. Picked up Pietri by the elbows and escorted him across the line – it looked like two burly, well-dressed bouncers giving the heave-ho to a half-dressed drunk.

(Question for the Press and the New England AAU:

If I was not an "amateur" – accusations that my managers, Rosenthal then Flanagan, took more than expense money and/or kicked back some of it to me – why did I turn down Alf Shrubb's 1907 offer of five races, at $1,000 per race, just so I could go to the Olympics?

Five. Ten. Fifteen. Twenty. Twenty-five miles. Seventy-five miles for $5,000. Do you think I got more than that to smash the American ten-mile record?)

It had to hurt Pietri, being disqualified. But Dorando was a runner, unwilling to overlook one yard let alone forty. On December 15 we had our first rematch, at Madison Square Garden, also (note to Press) my first "pro" race. Twenty-five thousand people stormed the Garden doors; firemen drove ten thousand away. Pietri had beaten Hayes three weeks before. We traded leads, back and forth, but this time Pietri collapsed with six laps to go, and I didn't. They brought him in by stretcher and we spoke in the locker room. "Tough miles, Dorando," I said to him. "Tough eenches, Tom," he answered. Only a week later, in Buffalo – and Lauretta and I just married in between – we ran a return match. Dorando stepped off the track at nineteen miles. *Eenches, Tom*, I heard as I walked-jogged home.

It was conceived as a ladder tournament. Now I got to tackle Shrubb.

January 26, 1909. The Shrubb-Longboat Marathon at Madison Square Garden was watched by twelve thousand people. Flanagan had just quit as my manager, selling my contract and puffing some smoke which the papers (typically) blew into flames. At the worst, Alfie had eight laps on me, but eventually it was he who tottered off the track. I tick-tocked in the roar for sixteen laps.

Professional Champion of the World.

What a season of races that was! None of us willing to leave anything on the track. Like boxers who won't settle for a decision. Knockouts only!

Nine years later, in France, it was a different game. As a despatch runner, I covered short distances, but the organizers had added obstacles of bullets and shells and barbed wire and craters. Mud and fog. You lost the field and ran entirely alone. If the fog got too thick, you were welcome to sleep overnight in a soggy field, no penalty except an aching back. And the goal was reversed from the golden years: since there were no winners, you prayed just to cross the finish line.

I ran hunched over, bent like a gnome, due to back wounds and the presence of guns.

Then one day, in Belgium, there was a magic like the spell that overtook me in London. Only with a much happier result. I had just jogged into an officers' communication trench when a shell exploded and buried all of us. It took me a few minutes to realize this. At first, all I felt was my knees buckle, my eyes go milky, and my head roar. *London*, I thought. Then, when I came to, and shook free of the dirt, there was blood – something warm and salty anyway (it was pitch black) – running from my nose. *London.*

But it was Belgium, and here was the miracle. No one in the trench was hurt, though we were good and buried. (It took some time to convince two boys that they hadn't been killed. They were clutching each other in a corner, moaning and shivering. Later, they put their hands down each other's flies and spent the next six days that way, still moaning and shivering.)

"Are we dead?" whispered a voice in the dark.

I started laughing. "No, boys, we're out of the race, and with any luck we'll stay out for a while."

We were getting air, somehow, and we had provisions for weeks. Of course, the smell of six men, close, got a little rich, and an overflowing latrine and the lovers carrying on . . . all in all, it was like most trenches. We slept twenty hours out of twenty-four and ate like hogs. When they "rescued" us, after six days underground, we must have looked like winter ground-hogs, blinking unwillingly at the light.

Still, that "death" cost me Lauretta, who for once believed the newspapers. I was already demobbed when, in 1919, I ran my last military race. Kicked out to win against Bill Queal in a three-miler at "The Grand Army of Canada Sports Show." I was thirty-two years old, and for fifteen minutes, the decade just past rolled back and never happened, or got ready to happen again.

~

On Training Methods, and my decision to quit the YMCA and join the Irish Club.

The Y felt that liquor and the company of women, even in moderation, were weakening for any man and disastrous for a runner.

I disagreed.

As did Tom Flanagan, hammer thrower and owner of the Grand Hotel.

As did Lauretta.

~

Evening Walks (II).

In the photo of Alf Shrubb and me, taken before our 1931 exhibition race, we look like what we are: a couple of old coots who used to be pro runners. Alf looks skinnier than ever, maybe sick. Me, in my white shorts and sleeveless undershirt, I *look* like a city worker who has just woken up and is leaning out his front door. What the paperboy must see Sunday morning when he comes to collect.

I don't remember who won.

It flashed on me that I'd agreed to enter the four-mile Jubilee run in Hamilton only on the condition that the first prize be a second-hand car, a '26 Chrysler. I was forty, just hired on by the City. Martha and the kids and I liked to drive out of town on the weekends, out to Ohsweken or just around. To lacrosse and wrestling matches. And it hit me in the moments after she fell – looking down at her and sprinting like hell – that probably none of that would change. That seemed very strange and awful: that this death could not alter our habits.

~

The Onondaga Wonder
The Streak of Bronze
The Caledonia Cyclone
Wildfire

My best run?

Hard to say. It might have been *almost* beating Higasadini's record for twelve miles.

Higasadini (Deerfoot), a Seneca, ran in moccasins in the 1850s and 1860s. Mother remembered hearing about him. In Hamilton, he and his partner Steep Rock won $1,000 by outrunning three horses in a ten-mile relay race. On his tour of England in 1863 he set a record for the one-hour run that would last for ninety years. In my training runs I sometimes took a poke at it. Grinding concession road into 3,600 second-grains, and draining them through the most pinch-waisted hourglass I could find. Telling no one, I found a white farmhouse that was exactly eleven miles distant from Mother's house, standing by itself in a field. Reaching it would have given me Deerfoot's record, plus a few yards to spare. But always, always, at the end of my run, my watch-hand jerked to 12 with the farmhouse still up ahead, starting to loom, but still a good ways off. I kept walking towards it as I cooled down, but out of superstition I always turned back before I reached it. Of all the roads I walked and ran, it was the only one that stopped me at eleven miles. In a way I'm just as glad.

Evening walks (III).

In one way, 1946 was like 1906, except that now it was Martha, not Mother, who disbelieved how far I walked.

When I checked myself out of Sunnybrook Hospital (they'd already told me I had diabetes, which was all they could do), I phoned Martha. A mistake. She was almost too angry to come and get me.

"What road are you coming in on?" I inquired, trying to make the question sound innocent.

My second mistake. She was as sharp as Lauretta in most ways.

"You stay right there," she hissed. "Don't move."

But I put down fifteen miles before I saw our Studebaker approaching. Henry Greene, our neighbour, was at the wheel; Martha no longer drove. Martha made a show of checking Henry's pocket-watch before she'd let me in the car.

"Good. You hitched a ride," she said, smiling grimly.

But if she really believed that, why did she make me sit in the back seat? "You're too sick to drive," she declared. And shot a glare at Henry who was grinning at me in the mirror.

"Drive," she told him.

A runner's strides are all to reach himself. That thought's occurred to me more than once, usually while running. As if, with enough speed and stamina, you could catch the front-runner who decides things before you know or act on them, and tap him on the shoulder. *Hey.*

(And suppose he turns his head: do you recognize him?)

Like when I wrote my protest letter to the *Hamilton Spectator* "to declare war on the cheap two-bit imposter who has been capitalizing on my famous name for the last fifteen to twenty years, by calling himself Tom Longboat for the purpose of obtaining free drinks in various beverage rooms."

I'd heard the story for years. At first it made me chuckle; rumours were nothing new, and they generally come in one shade: black. As time went on, it nagged a bit, something I'd have to get around to fixing, though there seemed no hurry.

What surprised me, when I finally put pen to paper, was my anger. Swiping the envelope flap across my tongue, mashing it sealed with my fist.

Naturally I thought of Doc. It'd been twenty years since we'd taken our midnight ramble through the Steel Company, along the tracks at Hamilton Bay, seen the pyramids of ore and coal,

Doc whispering, "Egypt." And Doc, I figured, who had the soul of a panhandler already – with his boy's scrapbook and old man's tears – maybe the tingle of spunk I'd slipped between his shoulder blades was all the push he needed to make him an aggressive one.

Roused up, I started rifling through the other pictures in Martha's cedar box, where I'd found the recent snap I'd sent the paper. She kept everything (unlike Lauretta, who was content to let the moment slide by), in a jumble of no particular order. Picture of me in a Maple Leaf singlet, hands loose-fisted at waist, looking more like a boxer than a runner. As a body under a blanket on a cart, being wheeled off the field by an official after I collapsed from sunstroke: Chicago, 1909. (And it occurs to me – for the first time, strangely – that Martha must've been keeping her own scrapbook, because we hadn't even met yet and I never saved these.) Alfie and I, lining up for Auld Lang Syne. Ghosting Shrubb in greener days. Flashing my "smile that won't come off" after beating Pietri in the indoor marathon. *The Indian Made a Pace the Italian Could Not Hold. "Bring on your next champion," dared the Canadian redman.* Grinning as I buy a newspaper from a kid in a trench in France – remember nothing of the day, the kid, or the big rangy guy grinning between us. Only the kid unsmiling.

Here's Lauretta and I on our honeymoon, looking starchy. The photographer was a prim and fussy individual whose flashbulbs kept popping; plus we weren't giving each other much sleep.

The two at the bottom must be thirty years apart. From my pro days: I relax in a wingback armchair, dressed to the nines in a fancy suit, sucking a fat cigar. Seventeen thousand dollars in winnings my first three years as a pro (Lauretta kept the accounts, entering it all in a slim red book with blue lines). Right behind it a more recent clipping from the *Star*: we see a placid old fellow in suspenders, smoking a thin-stemmed pipe, smiling benignly under a straw hat. One gloved hand at his side, the other reaching up to the heap on the truck, as if to pat some stray litter back into place. *Tom, Tom, the Garbage Man* – one neighbourhood kid kept trying to get my goat.

I stir through the pictures a while, to no particular purpose. But feeling restless, jazzed up. I keep coming back to the last two, holding them slightly apart in either hand, like bookends on a short shelf. It's not just that they look so different. Mother always maintained that anyone who looked the same in every photo was not a human being. I know that's so. But she also said you gain spirit by spending it, and here I'm not so sure. There I have to pause for a second. Because the fact is, the young lion at his ease in 1909, and the obliging codger circa 1940, not only don't look like each other, but I don't think they *are* the same man. And neither of them resembles the face I shave. For a few moments, sitting in our living room in Ohsweken, Martha off visiting somewhere, there is this mystery in the air that can't be explained or dispelled.

After the Boston, several thousand people met my train at Union Station. They gave me a torchlight parade, in the competing blare of three bands, up Bay Street to City Hall. There, Mayor Coatsworth presented me with a gold medal and a promise of $500 for my education. (Controller Hubbard had told the reception committee: "I have been thinking of the silver cabinets, etc., which other runners have received, and I have decided that they are not fitting for the young man who has practically no home but a boarding house.")

The *Daily Star* added this praise: "Canada makes no bones about gaining a little glory from an Indian. In other matters than footraces we have become accustomed to leaders from the Six Nations. We give the Boston papers notice, one and all, that we claim Longboat as a Canadian."

An additional $250.05 was raised by public subscription.

Later in 1907, I asked if the money, instead of being saved for my education, could be used to build a house for Mother. At first the board of control agreed, but when the American AAU started grousing about my amateur status again, the city treasurer decided to withhold the money until after the 1908 Olympics.

November, 1908. Flanagan requests the money be paid. The board of control authorizes it, but issues no cheque, and gives no explanation.

1909. I write. They cannot do it at this time.

1910. I write again. I am paid $50.

1911. I write again. The city sends $165 to Lauretta. (She agrees – privately – to buy me a box of cigars out of it.)

1912. I hire my first lawyer. He chases the city around the legal track. The city pays me the $35.05 remaining from public donations.

I never received the $500. Though it could never be said that I did not get an education.

Surprised Frank Montour, the wrestler and band councillor. He stopped to give me a lift on a cold night just after Christmas.

"No thanks," I said.

"Where have you been?" he asked.

"I've just had a nice walk to Hagersville."

Frank's mind going as he figured the distance. Close to twenty miles. He drove, I walked, back into Ohsweken.

I would be dead of pneumonia within two weeks.

In 1949, after a sojourn of sixty-one years, eleven years before my People got the vote, I was buried according to the dictates of the Great Spirit.

The women of my family hand-stitched the cotton and wool that they dressed me in. Two white fringed shirts and dark blue beaded trousers: Onondaga colours, the colours of my tribe. They tied a blue silk ribbon across my chest and draped a blue silk shawl over my shoulders and tied a silk bandana around my head. My daughter slipped new buckskin moccasins on my feet. The service was spoken in Onondaga, my sons leading the chants.

Henry Greene whittled a V in the top of the coffin to permit my spirit to escape. V less for Victory than for a runner's legs, upended, still.

He kept it small, mindful perhaps of Mother's favourite lesson: Be A Prodigal Soul.

Cogagwee.

My Greatest Race?

Maybe the one I lost to George Bonhag.

It was a three-mile match race in 1907 that I had no business running. Bonhag was the U.S. five-mile champ and he held the U.S. indoor three-mile record. I'd won my four races in 1906 in Hamilton and Toronto. I'd never run a short race before and I'd never raced indoors.

Nine thousand people paid to watch us.

Bonhag beat me by eight inches.

We both broke his record.

(Bonhag at the finish line beside me, both of us bent over double, hands on knees: "Goddamn, kid. God *damn*." His gasp of breath urgent as a lover's hiss.)

For a runner there is only the official version, the truth of legs, the clock's verdict. But a committee, composed of hereditary chiefs, speaks with many tongues, none of them ideally correct. Officially, the council of the Six Nations at Ohsweken refused to join the war. As a sovereign nation, historically allied to the British crown, they held out for a request for assistance from London. They were patient men.

Unofficially, women on the reserve raised money, knitted socks and sweaters, and made bandages. Men who enlisted were not disdained.

I was of two minds, too. I raced myself, alone, but when I chased Alf Shrubb, the Maple Leaf hung low over my diaphragm, a flaming at my middle. Alf wore the Union Jack higher, a cross with rays below his neck, on a dark singlet.

Attempts to shame were crude, but hardly ineffective.

The Issue is One of
CIVILIZATION vs. BARBARISM

*If civilization wins, Canadian people shall enjoy
their rights and privileges as heretofore.
If barbarism wins, Canadians will be placed in
German shackles.*

THE DUTY OF CANADIANS

*The participants in outside Canadian sport are mostly
unmarried men with few responsibilities, and with
years of vigorous athletic training, are the logical
individuals to defend the honour of the nation.*

"Logical?" Lauretta jeered. "Ask the women what's logical. They might say leave the young fit men here. Send the fat married ones first."

"I'm married," I tried a grin.

"Yes, *you* are," she said softly, but with that sternness. Like Mother, I could see then. I don't know how I missed it before.

Six months later, when I enlisted, I was trying to get up nerve to tell her. We were sitting in the house at Ohsweken, smoking and drinking. Clock ticking. Lauretta's talk had a more corrosive edge than usual, brittle, like she'd touched acid or frost. She was a sensitive woman. When a bee passed she felt the shock wave, a tiny slap of honey or death.

The worst of it was, I didn't have a reason I could tell her (which needn't have bothered me, since *why* paled beside *what* to Lauretta). The pro running circuit had been drying up since 1912. I was twenty-nine. Near the close of youth (I realize now), men are prey to wild crusades, a target for that poised nerve and muscle.

"This is just stupid," Lauretta said.

I crossed the living room, a long distance it seemed, and stood beside her chair. Looked down where her thumb, hard-shelled like a beetle, lay alongside another advertisement.

"WHY DON'T
THEY COME?"

WHY BE A MERE SPECTATOR HERE
WHEN YOU SHOULD PLAY A <u>MANS</u> PART
IN THE REAL GAME OVERSEAS?

Lauretta snorted softly. "They spelled 'man's' wrong."

Did they? It seemed Lauretta had even more contempt for the minds behind the war than for the war. But I thought the minds were adequate. They did not dissuade me through foolishness, made foolishness irrelevant. In my mind I'd already moved closer to the soldier in the picture, with his pack and rifle and boots and bandaged head, silhouettes of artillery cannons puffing smoke behind him. Had already shifted from the fantasy blooming in the smoke from his rifle barrel, fans waving hats at toy figures playing hockey. I was ready to go, had gone.

Lauretta looked up and saw. She didn't say anything. Just opened her brown eyes wide and looked at me, long and hard, then narrowed them; she did that several times, as if her eyes were a camera and she were taking my photograph. My perspective whirled, and I felt she was looking down at me. And I felt that she was measuring my face to remember it after it was dead and still.

Truth was stranger. I would come back from the dead to find her married, happily, to another man. "Tom, you're back," she said. It was an accusation.

Walking. The sportswriters used to marvel when I told them my training consisted of daily walks, of fifteen to twenty miles, with a couple of fast timed runs per week. Even in this, they suspected me of lying. One scribe waxed eloquent: "Could this modest regimen really produce those prodigious feats of stamina and speed we have been privileged to witness?"

Answer: yes.

But he wouldn't have believed me. And – in a way – perhaps he was right to be sceptical. For me, walking went far beyond a key to success in sport. It was my way of life, my life.

I discovered it accidentally, and in defeat. The way most true things are found.

After I left the Institute, I was a running fiend. From twelve to eighteen, I ran every chance I got, my legs two long itches only speed could scratch. I'd run from crosses and pale droning spinsters, painted Saints, and sour-smelling scribblers, hours spent communing with the ghosts of Pauline Johnson and Joseph Brant, my farting rear to the classroom. Running could take me away from everything, I believed. And this was true.

Heading out to jobs as a farm labourer in houses off the reserve, I tore up road. I walked only with the greatest reluctance, a penance I paid to scorched lungs and swampy legs. There were canneries in Caledonia and Hagersville, Hamilton, Brantford and Burlington, where I picked up seasonal work. I ran (and walked), ran (and walked), to and from all of them.

I watched the road races on field days and in the Highland Games. Knowing – knowing-dreaming – I would be part of them soon.

Bill Davis was my hero then. A Mohawk from Ohsweken, he'd won races all over Ontario. In 1901, he'd finished second in the Boston Marathon. "That close," he said, his hands straddling a length of air.

In the spring of 1905, just before my eighteenth birthday, I decided it was my time. My legs wouldn't let me wait any longer. I entered the annual Victoria Day five-mile race in Caledonia.

When the starter's gun cracked, I sprang into the wind, the Institute behind me. The rest is easy to tell. I ran too fast, burning myself up, and in the last half mile, someone passed me.

I was unhappy and happy. I had run my first race. My second-place silver medal, which I fingered in my pocket as I walked home, could not but turn to gold. I was eighteen. More strength lay ahead of me.

The walk home was almost five miles, too. I walked it fast, and sometimes I broke into a scornful sprint, just to show the speed I had to waste. After one such run, I stopped, gasping, beside a field of tall grasses. From the field came a giant hum, a churn of rampant life, which I could not separate into the sound of individual insects. It seemed more the sizzle of growing, of life itself. Breezes passed through the grass like blushes through skin. Clouds sent cool bobbling shadows over the field and me. And there was the buzzing, like a tiny roar, the crackle of a fire breaking out, everywhere.

Cogagwee, I thought. Me, my name. *Everything.*

Excited, I leaped over the ditch to be closer to the buzzing grass. I stood in it, the sharp blades scratching my legs. I passed my hands over the frizzy, flowering tops, wondering if the pubic hair of women, which I had not felt yet, felt this way, soft yet dry, pleasantly prickly.

I saw a black dot near the base of a long stalk of grass, and stooped to look at it. It must have been a type of beetle, it was black, but though I peered at it closely, no other details of its appearance have remained with me, only its motion. I remember touching it with my finger. It stopped climbing. I touched it again, a gentle nudge. Now its six legs scrambled forward – it ran – but only for a short distance. Then it walked again.

Several times I did this – touched the black beetle to see it stop or run – while I felt an idea growing inside me, my stomach prickling with excitement from the beetle's lesson.

Running and stopping are the same, you do them *from* something. Walking is life, is time, it takes you *towards*.

The secret churned my stomach, ached along my limbs.

I walked to Dunnville and back, fifty miles. "Don't lie," Mother said, "or you'll find another house."

My brother took a horse and buggy to Hamilton. I gave him a half-hour lead, then met him on King Street. His jaw fell open. "Does Mother know?" he asked. I think at that moment he believed me capable of anything: of flying, of telepathy, of spirit-walking. I just grinned at him.

Next Victoria Day, at Caledonia, I walked to the start line. Felt the touch, a tap, a flick, between my shoulder blades. Ran a short way along the stalk and won easily. Resumed walking, and walked slowly home.

Unattributed newspaper quotations are taken from *The Globe*. Much of the factual material was found in *Tom Longboat*, Bruce Kidd's short, vivid account of the runner's life and career, which also guided me back to newspaper stories of the time.

ROBERT McGILL

Confidence Men

"We could've skunked'um, Cam. You should've just stayed out of it and watched us skunk'um."

"Oh yeah?" she replies. "That split lip you got there tells a different story, Mr. Man." Then they really start into her and she is laughing all through it, she can't help it. They always get angry when she calls them Mr. Man. That's why she does it: it's funny when they puff themselves up and act insulted. They aren't, though, not really. The only time they hate it is when their uncle or somebody calls them by it, too, just to avoid figuring out which one is which. But Cam is good. She can tell Seamus from Sean a block away, even with their same floppy blond hair, and even when they try to trick her by dressing up like each other. That always backfires anyhow, because they have ridiculous ideas about how the other one acts and they overplay their parts. Sean starts swinging his arms as though Seamus were an orangutan, and Seamus changes his voice so that Sean sounds vaguely like he is from a breakaway Soviet republic. Perhaps it will be harder once they get older and more subtle. Or perhaps they will go different ways. Maybe they will hate each other and decide to make it so that nobody ever gets them mixed up again.

Everyone wants to know how she does it. They'll never ask her straight out, but when they're in the same room with her and the boys, she can feel them watching her, trying to pick up on some little trick. And sooner or later, when the twins are upstairs or outside, they'll ask: "So what's your secret?" She gives a different answer each time: Seamus has one ear slightly bigger than the other. Sean's voice always goes up at the end of his sentences. Little things which no one can dispute, but which they can't themselves identify. The truth is, she doesn't know how she does it. It used to bother her, this unknowing. It made her worry that eventually the skill might just slip away. For a while she tried to pay attention to their mannerisms, to figure out exactly how she knew. But she gave up. Either her instincts are more developed than her ability to make sense of them, or some part of her wants to preserve the mystery of her talent.

She carries her trumpet case in her right hand and swings it a little as she goes, remembering the morning's band practice. Mr. Werther had been anxious. There were bags under his eyes and his hair was sticking up everywhere like he'd just rolled out of bed. This was not unusual, and they were all patient, knowing that sooner or later they'd probably find out what was bothering him. Sure enough, he made a cut-off signal – like he was swatting at a deerfly – in the middle of leading them through some scales, and he asked them if their parents had been to many concerts. There was mumbling, some shaking and nodding of heads. Mr. Werther seemed to take this to confirm his worst suspicions. The year-end music festival was only a week away, and the band was playing the first two movements of *The Planets*. Mr. Werther was afraid that the audience would think the piece was over when the first movement had ended. You weren't supposed to clap between the movements, said Mr. Werther. Did their parents know that? He would keep his hands held up and his baton at the ready to show the audience that the piece was not done. Would they understand this signal?

One of the clarinets asked if the pause between the movements was like an intermission where you could get up and go to the bathroom. Mr. Werther said loudly that it was not. He ran his fingers through his hair and then yanked his hand away, as though it had touched fire, when it came to the bits that were sticking up.

Tuesday, the day when Cam gets up early for band practice, always seems the longest. As soon as her last class finished this afternoon she ran to her locker and then walked down the hill to the elementary school to pick up the boys. She entertained a lazy notion of detouring along the main street to Jodi's to see if they had any new tanktops come in, but it was too warm to walk more than necessary. The air was still heavy with a stubborn refusal to rain and the tree shadows were just beginning to creep across the street. Early June is the time of year, Cam thought, when there is too much school left and everything you want to buy is full price.

Seamus and Sean weren't at the meeting-place by the lamppost out front where the school buses made their pickups, so she walked around the building. When she finally found them in the south yard they were standing back-to-back and there was a whole pack surrounding them. She got there just in time to see Seamus take one on the mouth from Cole Mitchell, and then she was wading into the middle where she peeled the bunch of them away like a paring knife, her trumpet case abandoned on the tarmac near the tetherball pole. The pack regrouped and said she was a bitch and a lezzie and one of them threw a rock half-heartedly when they were at a safe distance, but she had four years and half a foot on the oldest of them and they knew from past bruises that they couldn't push her too far.

Now the twins are talking energetically and laughing in front of her. Sometimes they will lean over to one another and place a head on a shoulder as they walk, or squeeze hands. Alone with Cam as they are now, they fall into it naturally, but at school it is happening less and less, and when they do, it is with hard, darting eyes. They are daring someone to say something, waiting for it. Perhaps that's how things started today in the schoolyard. Nothing has been said about what happened. Nothing ever is. She doesn't have to ask to know.

It's been like this ever since they came to town and started living with Cam and her parents. The news about what had happened to their mother got spread around before they arrived, of course. Aunt Melissa had grown up in town, everyone remembered her, everyone was horrified to hear the public reports and the private rumours. That didn't stop anybody from talking about it, though. Cam has even heard them do it, in the donut shop or in the supermarket before they see her standing in the aisle. They seem to get pleasure in sharing the details, always in the most apologetic tones. She has watched as they wait to see the shock that they know the story will bring. They will have known Aunt Melissa just enough for their horror to be genuine, but just barely enough that they can get a good gory scare from repeating the story, feel like adults for pretending that it's all very confidential and disgusting, and then go to sleep that night without another thought. Somewhere along the line the story has been passed down to the children, maybe when somebody took his son along on a fishing trip with buddies – maybe a man with a secret wish to do the same thing he was talking about! – or just as likely it was one of those mothers who has gone claustrophobic from spending all day with the laundry and the kids, who's made them her confidants, telling them about other people's miseries to teach them a life lesson or get more love.

Eventually it filtered down to the schoolyard where there was no discretion at all.

The Philipses' house is at the end of Frank Street, four blocks from the elementary school. The three of them walk in through the back porch to the kitchen and her mother is there preparing dinner, the windows open as far as possible to let out the steam from the potato pot. Cam watches as her mother glances from one boy to the other. Mrs. Philips doesn't even notice the lip at first; she's too busy figuring out who's who. Most days she insists on helping them dress, enduring endless protests so that she can get them into colours she will remember, but this morning she took Cam to band practice and missed her chance. She seems to be starting a second going-over when she finally sees.

"Oh, Sean, look at you! What happened to your face?" exclaims Mrs. Philips. The boy shrugs and the two of them walk slowly past her into the television room, as though compelled. Cam moves to follow but is called back. "Did he get in a fight again?" her mother demands.

"Wasn't any fight," says Cam. "Bunch of them were ganging up on Mr. Men. Just for something to do."

"These things don't just happen," says her mother. "Somebody must have said something. Do you know what it was? Were they teasing them about – you know, about Aunt Melissa?" She doesn't mention Uncle Tony. No one says his name anymore.

"Maybe," Cam says. "I got there too late to hear." She's thinking that it isn't teasing at all. More like torture, maybe. "But Mom," she adds. "That was Seamus, not Sean."

Cam leaves for the television room and convinces Seamus to let her clean his lip and put a bandage on the skin just below. Then she returns to the kitchen and, without being asked, begins to help her mother with dinner. Mrs. Philips is always tired now that the twins are in the house. She is used to one child. Cam remembers arguments, some of them not too long before Sean and Seamus arrived, when her mother would storm away into Mr. Philips's den and declare, loudly so that Cam would hear, "Thank God we had the sense to stop after one! She's going to send me to an early grave." Cam's father, on the other hand, does not seem so disturbed by the presence of the two boys. He plays soccer with them in the back yard, he goes to Meet the Teacher night and talks with the woman who runs the grade-two class and with the psychologist who works in the county schools. It's the Philips blood that the boys share, not Mrs. Philips's. Cam thinks that this must make it easier for her father to love them. Her mother has to work at it.

Mrs. Philips is preparing a meatloaf. She has been wrestling with the ketchup bottle, squeezing it until her fingers blanch and then spanking it harder and harder over the mixing bowl. Now she hands the bottle to Cam, who has been watching with a disapproving look. "All right, go ahead and try it," says Mrs. Philips with a half-smile. She remembers that Cam has recently demonstrated a new method for getting the last stubborn bits out of containers. Cam learned it in science class. Mrs. Philips laughed when she saw Cam do it before and said how that was quite the trick.

Cam takes the bottle in both hands, the neck pointing away from her, and begins to spin it wildly in a motion as close to a circle as the angles of her body will allow.

"Centrifugal force! Centrifugal force!" she cries as she turns. It is a habit Cam has picked up lately: naming such things as she invokes them. To her it feels like she is using some recently discovered power, a new and secret way of seeing the world, an intimacy with its hidden springs and mechanisms. "First law of momentum," she will shriek as she coasts on her bike past the cemetery at the bottom of the Elm Street hill. Or she'll peek her head into her father's den where he is sleeping on the couch and wake him, bellowing "The inertia principle!" and then cackling wickedly. His eyes pop open and he scowls, but Cam has her mother on her side: "You shouldn't have been napping in the first place, it's seven o'clock for heaven's sake."

Cam can feel the ketchup slide away from the bottom of the bottle as it spins. "Enough, enough," says her mother, but Cam is having fun, she twirls faster and faster. Then something happens which she did not expect. The pressure pops open the plastic cap, and ketchup goes spraying across the kitchen. In the half-second before she brings the bottle to a halt, most of its contents are splattered across the tablecloth, the chairs, the yellow window curtains.

"I'm sorry. I'm sorry," she is pleading before her mother has even fully turned around. Cam reseals the lid on the bottle, then sets it on the counter and reaches for a roll of paper towels.

"Damn it, Cam, I told you enough, didn't I?" says her mother. "No, don't bother trying to scrub it off, you'll just make it worse." She makes a vaguely menacing motion towards her daughter and Cam deferentially retreats to lean against the counter. But this too is wrong, she can never do anything right after mistakes like these. "Don't just stand there, help me lift this out of the way, quickly in case one of the boys walks in." After that there is very little talking; both know the urgency of cleaning up before Sean or Seamus come into the kitchen. Mrs. Philips takes a quick glance into the television room and comes back with a mildly placated expression; they are busy watching their four-thirty program. "But God knows when there'll be a commercial and they'll wander in here looking for something to eat," she says. "Here, help me get the curtains, too. We'll throw it all in the wash."

A few minutes later everything is done except the floor, and they are down on their knees trying to work yellow sponges around the chair and table legs without making too much noise.

Mrs. Philips whispers through gritted teeth. "I don't know if I should even bother asking this, but weren't you supposed to get a math test back today?"

"Yes. I did all right." Cam knows this response will not be enough to satisfy her mother.

"What does 'all right' mean?" Mrs. Philips says. She has decided to stop whispering. "Did you pass?"

"Fifty-seven."

"Fifty-seven," repeats her mother flatly, like she is speaking a number she has never heard before. "How do you ever expect to get to university with those kinds of grades?" Cam shrugs and says nothing. Three years of high school still to go and already her mother can speak about nothing but university. She hangs it over Cam's head as though making it there is the same as getting into heaven. No, not heaven. More like a negative hell. "What's it going to be like if you stay in this town all your life?" is what her mother always wants to know, but her mother already seems to have a good idea of the answer. Cam is not so sure. It's not such a bad place, this town. This is not such a bad family. "You sure won't be living in this house, I can tell you that, young lady." That warning worries Cam a bit, makes her think about things. Maybe she could wait tables at the Chinese restaurant. Then she could rent one of the upstairs apartments overlooking the main street. The schools would only be five minutes away.

When all the red is gone from the floor, they both stand up at the same time. Cam bends over to rub her knees but finds herself lifted by her mother's arms, which slip in under hers and pull her close.

"Thanks for helping to clean up. I'm sorry to be such a grouch today." Mrs. Philips's voice is tired, conciliatory.

"Don't worry about it, Mom." Cam is still shocked by these sudden, unpredictable reversals. They are something she has grown to expect from her friends, but they seem strange and disturbing in an adult. Has her mother always acted like this, or is it something Cam has just never noticed before? This is the kind of question Cam finds herself asking all the time, in the same way that she has decided that at some point, maybe it was grade six or seven, she started coming in from playing tag or football during the recess with the awareness that she was sweating. She could feel it beading on her forehead and the back of her neck; taking deep, surreptitious breaths through her nose, she could detect the odour of her own body. She sat at her desk under the fluorescent lights and felt as though everyone in the class must be able to see the dark liquid marks on her shirt, must be able to smell her. What was happening? She had always run around at recess. Had she never sweated before? Or was this only part of a new self-awareness, a new paranoia? When the twins had moved in, that was one of the first things she had watched for in them: sweat. They seemed not to produce it at all. Maybe boys were different from girls.

Her mother releases her, takes the sponge Cam has been holding in her hand throughout the embrace, and throws it in the sink. Then she reaches into the cupboard for a new ketchup bottle. Cam decides that she is no longer needed in the kitchen, or perhaps only no longer wanted there, and goes into the television room. Sean is directly in front of the screen, watching a commercial for a remote-controlled car.

"Haven't you seen that one before, buddy?" she says. He screws up his face as though she has just said the dumbest thing imaginable.

"They show it every time there's commercials," he complains. "Watch, I'll turn it off and do all the words for you."

"Nah, that's okay," she says. "But you're sitting way too close. Back her up a bit, fella." Then she asks, "Where's Seamus gone to, anyway?"

"He went to get something to eat. I thought he was with you guys," says Sean. His eyes never move from the television screen. "Shhh, it's back on." Cam is already heading up the stairs.

He is not in the twins' room, not in her room. Then she hears the water running in the bathroom. She knocks on the door, a little harder than she intends.

"Seamus, you okay in there?" The water shuts off. There is no reply. "Seamus?" She begins to knock harder and skins her knuckles when the door opens. He is standing there behind it, looking up blankly.

"Ya, what?" he says. So that's it, she hopes. Just going to the toilet.

"You're missing your show," she observes. He shrugs.

"I'd rather hear you read to me," he says. She smiles with relief.

"Okay! What you want to hear? Some more Mr. Men?" He nods and they go off to the twins' room. He picks out one of the books – there are about a hundred and they're all short; thankfully neither of the boys seems to have a favourite or it would be a continual battle to get them to choose one of the others – and sits next to her as she reads. No comments, no cuddling. Perhaps he saw the kitchen after all.

A part of her wants him to confess. Besides bits of gossip, all she knows about what really happened came from the newspaper during Uncle Tony's trial, before her mother saw the article and threw out the paper, then cancelled their subscription. Some nights the boys wake up screaming and when Cam comes to them and turns on the lights, they are sitting up in the bed with the covers kicked to the floor, still clutching their heads, each of them with his hands over his ears like he is trying to keep his brains from spilling out. She crawls into bed with them and holds them, watching the shadows of her parents as they lurk silently outside the room before padding down the hall. The boys always fall asleep ahead of her, always within seconds of each other, and it is the rhythm of their paired breathing that eventually lulls her out of consciousness. The next day no one says anything about it. The only time it comes out is with the psychiatrist, when the boys are off in the hospital play area and there are a few minutes when Mr. and Mrs. Philips are there and the doctor has not yet asked Cam to leave the room. She has never protested these expulsions. She thinks it is all ridiculous, anyway.

Only Sean saw it happen, right in front of his eyes. That's what the psychiatrist thinks, although both of them have the dreams and neither of them will talk about it. But it's Seamus who is acting strangely, Mr. and Mrs. Philips point out (only knowing to say this, Cam thinks, because she has told them). He refuses to eat, he starts at noises and sudden movements, sometimes he goes for hours without saying anything. The psychiatrist says it's because they're twins. Seamus is used to understanding what Sean feels, but in this instance he can't share in the memory, so he's compensating with strange behaviour. He's trying to bridge the gap that he feels between them by taking on the experience, the memory.

"So he's just acting?" says Mr. Philips, and the psychiatrist nods reluctantly.

"Something like that."

Her parents have told the psychiatrist that Cam is closest to them, and every session he asks her if the boys have confided in her at all.

"Confided?" she repeated the first time. "You mean, told me something in confidence?" The psychiatrist blinked. Well, yes, he said. Is there anything he should know? She shook her head with regret. She wished she did have something to keep in confidence, but they really hadn't said a word, they still haven't. Sometimes Cam thinks that she almost wants them to break down a bit, for one of them to say to her, "I saw'm do it, Cam. I saw'm do it with the baseball bat." Then she would go to him and hold him, and the other one would come in, too. She would prefer if it were Seamus who said it. It would prove the doctor wrong, for one thing. But also, it would be too odd if Sean were to do it; Sean who is more sociable with other children, who will turn away from hugs when he is watching the television, who doesn't seem to need anyone, not even Seamus, sometimes.

After she and Seamus have finished the book, he asks to be read another, but she sends him downstairs to the television. Then she goes to her room and picks up the phone. She talks for almost an hour, until her mother calls her to dinner. When the meal is done and everyone has left the kitchen, she tells them that she is going for a walk. This is part of the truth. She is actually going to meet Peter Gretzky, out near the town reservoir.

The Gretzky family has been in the area for more than eighty years, quietly making its living on a beef farm south of town. Only in the last couple of decades, with the youngest generation of Gretzkys, have people taken any notice of them. It is all because of the name, of course. There is no relation, the family has insisted from the start, but it is such an uncommon name that most people just assume. None of the Gretzkys had ever played hockey – in fact, that antisocial behaviour was once their main claim to fame – but enough people kept saying things to Tadeusz Gretzky, Peter's father, that the man went to the hardware store and spent most of the money in his chequing account on equipment for the youngest boy, Leo. Then he sent him off to try out for the local rep team. Leo's mother thought she would save a few dollars by dressing him in a handed-down Edmonton Oilers jersey, since it had the right name, but the other players couldn't stop teasing him about it and the parents in the stands were always making smart comments about the number on the back. Mrs. Gretzky refused to buy Leo a different uniform, but it got so that he wasn't speaking to her anymore after games, he'd just go to his room and fantasize about meeting Wayne Gretzky and exacting some horrible revenge, and so eventually she tore out the stitching and sewed on a seven, instead. You could still see the little holes in an outline where the two nines had been. The hockey coach tried to milk the name, too: he'd start Leo at centre to get the other team worked up. This intimidation only lasted until the whistle went, though. Leo had none of his namesake's ability and took all the abuse. He was small and slow and clumsy, and every game there were a dozen players who wanted to say that they'd bodychecked Gretzky, they'd high-sticked Gretzky, they'd knocked Gretzky to the ice and left him bleeding in a broken lump.

Peter Gretzky has sympathy for his little brother but is glad it was not him. He swears that he is going to change his name as soon as he turns eighteen.

Cam tries her best to sympathize. "There's a Marilyn Munro who lives over in Hepworth," she pointed out once. "No 'e' at the end of the name, though," she added. Peter just grunted. He has little patience for such coincidences and confusions. He gets angry when a thing turns out to be different than he thought it was; he is always on guard for possible mix-ups. If Cam tries to tell him about something that happened and it sounds even vaguely implausible, if it's a rumour about the priest at the Catholic church or an episode that happened in a bar, he always interrupts right at the start. "Wait. Is this a story or is this a joke?" he wants to know.

It's different with Cam. She sees her life as a book that she is writing, a story with dozens of characters and plot twists, and she has to keep a close eye on all of them. The heroes of the story are her and Sean and Seamus. She has told Peter that this is how she thinks of things, and she has the feeling that Peter would like to be one of the heroes, too. This is what she is afraid of. She worries that one day she is going to have to say to Peter, I'm sorry. There is no more room in this story for anyone else.

Peter and Cam sit on the grass outside the chain-link fence that surrounds the reservoir and she tells him about the ketchup.

"It's silly, worrying about what they might do when we don't even know. I was almost hoping that Sean would walk in, so we could see. Maybe he'd just pick up another sponge and help."

"Why Sean?" Peter wants to know.

She admits to him that she has a preference. Then she finds herself saying something she never thought she'd say: how sometimes, to try to like Sean more, she'll pretend he's Seamus. She's learned to disassociate the person from the name. She acts like there are two Seamuses, but one of them she calls Sean.

It doesn't work, of course. Sean is nothing like Seamus.

Peter doesn't understand. "They're your cousins. You're supposed to like them the same."

"I love both the Mr. Men," she says loudly. "But everybody has their favourites, don't they?" Peter shrugs, and Cam can't believe it. She begins interrogating him. Wouldn't he rather spend time with one of his brothers more than the rest? He doesn't know. He says he's never thought of it like that. Cam is annoyed.

"Well of course, you're not *supposed* to think of it like that. But everybody does."

She notices Peter's hand slowly edging towards hers. She doesn't understand. They are arguing right now, doesn't he know that? He has never held her hand before, it wouldn't make any sense to start now. She lifts her hand from where it's been on the grass and rests it on her knee. His arm stops moving and he turns his head to look out over the reservoir. They talk about the field party that happened last week and what people did there – Peter went but Cam wasn't allowed, not until next year. Then he heads off on his bicycle and she begins to walk back towards town.

She gets to the house in time to help the boys into their pajamas. Then she reads to them from the Book of Amazing Advertisements. It is just a sketch pad with blank pages, but she tells them that she has X-ray eyes; she can read things that they can't even see. First she tells them about Crispo Cereal. It has no vitamins, no minerals, and in fact, no cereal; just a big prize in every box. Then she reads to them about Go-Go Roller Skates, which do all the tricks for you. She starts to name the tricks and they interrupt her when she leaves one out. "Oh, I must have misread that," she says, and they giggle. But their favourite is Bupso Soap. "Bupso Soap!" she cries, like a circus barker. "It doesn't wash, and it doesn't lather! It just keeps you company in the bath tub!" Then she sets aside the book and pretends to splash them. She is glad the day can end like this.

When it happens two weeks later, there is no ketchup and no teasing. The school year has finished for the boys the previous day. They want to ride on the teeter-totter; she is going to walk with them up to the park. Sean is in the downstairs toilet, and Seamus is with Cam in the mud room, chewing an apple. He bends over to tie his shoelaces and the juice comes running in a stream through his nose. Something that could happen to anybody. She is ready to go and has been flipping through a magazine; she only looks over when she hears the juice trickle onto the tiled floor. There is a second's pause, and then he is standing up, clawing at his own face. She has to grab his arms and hold them down, but he won't stop screaming. When Sean steps out of the bathroom, she yells at him to go find her mother, but he doesn't. He sees her pinning Seamus to the floor and he comes running at her, hits her full-force on her side and sends her falling until she takes the tile on her shoulder. Sean is biting and scratching and tearing at her clothing. She doesn't let go of Seamus even when her mother comes and pulls Sean from her, only when Mr. Philips arrives and holds the boy's arms for her.

At the moment that her father comes into the mud room, she is remembering a story she read to the twins about the Greek wrestler who dared any man to try to pry a pomegranate from his fingers. No one could, and when he finally opened his hand, everyone saw that the fruit was still unbruised. That is how she is trying to hold Seamus.

Later, when it has been a few weeks and they are still keeping watch on him at the hospital, she begins to make mistakes. She and Sean are in her room playing hide and seek. "Where are you?" she is saying. It is all for show: she knows where he is, she could hear him hiding in the closet. Then she says it: "Where could you be, Seamus?"

In more than a year living with both of them she never did that, not a single time. Now, the other one is not even around to cause any confusion and here she is slipping up, not once but twice in two days. The first time she did it, the error surprised them both so much that they stood there sharing exactly the same wide eyes and open mouth. Then gradually her face paled into a firm, adult stoicism: the resolve of realizing a mistake and refusing to acknowledge it. His faced changed, too. It hardened and his eyes flamed up, like a fire that she had started, that he was using to burn her, deep in his brain. Now, he has emerged from the closet, and that fire is back. This time it melts the determination she has been about to try on again. "Mr. Man!" she cries. "I didn't mean to call you that. Sean!"

She runs to him and throws her arms around his little body, rubbing his back furiously as though he were hypothermic. His arms stay stiffly at his side, but then they reach up and grip her awkwardly, both his hands on her spine, slightly offset so that one is not quite touching the other.

She remembers a night at the end of May: She is lying on her back with them in their bed, staring at the plastic stars that her father glued to the ceiling the day before the boys moved in. They're in the shape of constellations: Ursa Minor, Libra, Orion with his belt. In the daylight they are pale yellow, barely visible, but in the darkness they glow brightly.

"Are they stars or planets?" Sean asks, now that the shrieking is over, now that both are warm and nestled at her sides.

"Stars," says Seamus, a just-begun yawn elongating the word.

"I wasn't askin' you, I was askin' Cam," says Sean.

"He's right, Mr. Man," she says. "See, they've got those points on them. They're stars."

"Uncle Steven said that you can tell stars from planets 'cause stars twinkle. Those ones don't twinkle," says Sean.

"The real ones do, honey," says Cam, and strokes the top of his head. She falls asleep soon after, and doesn't stir when they crawl out of bed in the morning, not until she hears a creak and they are standing in the doorway, still wearing their pajamas.

"Good morning, Cam! Are you awake, Cam?" She waits for a moment, then lifts her head and smiles.

"You bet." They come running to the bed, jump on it and throw themselves on her, both hugging her at the same time.

"Will you read to us?" asks Sean, pulling back to look her in the eye gravely, as though he believes that this is the most important question he will ask all day. She laughs.

"Sure," she says. "Well, Mr. Man, who are you gonna be this time?" she wants to know, and she ruffles one's hair and then the other's. They bounce off the bed and go sliding to the bookshelf, knocking the whole series on the floor trying to pick one out. Mr. Happy. Mr. Forgetful. Mr. Prudent. They have so many choices.

NICK MELLING

Philemon

The family is sitting at the kitchen table. For the most part, they are motionless. Certainly they are silent. The chamber has the air of a hospital waiting room, both in the grimness of its inhabitants and the sterility of their surroundings.

They have almost finished their dinner: meat loaf and mashed potatoes. It has been Tuesday's fare as long as anyone can remember. By now the family sees the meal as a perennial menace, like the weekly visits of Jehovah's Witness ambassadors. But changing the routine would mean inventing a replacement, so they stoically consume the dismal food without leaving too much on their plates.

There are three of them at the table tonight. There have been three since the departure of Joanna, who fled for a land where meat loaf does not come back to haunt the house every Tuesday. There is also a dog, a black lab who lies under the table. He has been with them for many years, and no longer hopes for edible gifts to come his way.

The father of the house is a squat man with large glasses encircling small piggy eyes. He is the only member of the family still eating: a task which he does with great speed and skill, having had much practice.

His companion is sitting across the table from him. It is she who has concocted the meat loaf, though she has eaten little of it. She sits with her elbow on the table and her chin in her hand, regarding the rest of the family impassively.

Their son is half-sitting, half-lying in his chair. His feet rest on the body of the dog under him. He is waiting for the word of dismissal from either of his parents, one of the few disciplinary habits that has stood the test of time. No one can leave the table until everyone is finished eating. In the meantime, he amuses himself by tossing peas one by one into a water glass. Although this task requires more athletic effort than the son is usually willing to exert, it has the pleasant side effect of annoying his father, who regards all games involving food as sacrilegious.

Discerning his son's intent, the father retaliates by slowing his pace of eating. He begins to chew his food with feline care, leaving long pauses between each swallow.

During one of these breaks, he asks his son, "Do you want any more meat loaf?" There is a gloating gleam in his eye.

The son turns the glass on its side, presenting a horizontal target. He is now flicking the peas into it. "I think your need is greater than mine, Dad."

"Then I'll have another piece. And could you pass the peas?" There is triumph in the father's tone.

Undaunted, the son begins to pass the peas, one at a time, to his father. Most do land on his plate: the son has become an expert.

Abruptly, the silent mother speaks. "You can go." Her husband bestows on her the look of a betrayed child. Their son gives them both a warm smile, a victorious general accepting surrender. He slides off his chair and out of the room, followed by the black lab.

The father puts the meat loaf he has taken back onto the serving plate. He and his wife sit in silence.

"Cliff Allen's father died today," he ventures at last. "He had a heart attack, and died."

"He was in his nineties," his wife observes.

"In fifty years, we'll be in our nineties."

The wife is silent. She cannot argue with this.

"In forty years, we'll be in our eighties." The husband has found a reliable vehicle for conversation.

The wife stands up. Left without an audience for his predictions, her husband does the same. Dinner is over.

The son is in his room. He is reading a book. This is an unusual pastime for him, especially in summer when he regards every academic activity as a waste of time. There are very few activities, in fact, that he does not see in this light. His dog is sitting beside him on the bed. The dog views sedentary activity as a waste of time, but is far too polite to tell this to the boy. They waste twenty minutes together, in silence.

The phone rings. The boy waits until the third tone, then answers.

"Speaking," he says.

"What?" says his caller.

"Speaking."

There is a pause.

"Is your mom or dad home?" the caller asks.

"I don't know."

Another pause.

"Maybe I'll call back later," the caller says at last.

"Maybe you will," the boy agrees. The caller hangs up.

He returns to his book. Rarely does the boy read in a linear fashion; he chooses paragraphs at random from various pages. Right now, he is reading from somewhere in the middle of the book:

July 17th today we went to see egerdon castle which doesn't actually exist anymore but is still a great tourist attraction and it's really quite comical to see these crowds of people gaping in awe at the grassy hill on which egerdon castle used to stand before it was destroyed by thoughtless barbarians a thousand years ago but i guess it wasn't too funny because my whole goddam family was there gaping with the best of them actually i lied when i said the castle doesn't exist anymore because it does in part there's almost three feet of wall still standing and they've encircled it with a chainlink fence just in case the thoughtless barbarians might be lurking outside waiting for a chance to finish the job anyway after we'd finished

*staring reverently at the wall inside the chain link fence we got
in the car and drove away the way we'd come and that pretty
much sums up my day.*

It is not the first time the boy has indulged in perusing
Joanna's journal. It is more interesting than most of the other
books he reads, although he himself is rarely mentioned in it as
any more than a part of Joanna's goddam family.

The boy's parents are washing the dishes. Such grim work
invariably breeds grim conversation.

"I think I'm going to die before I reach my nineties," the
husband confesses.

"Probably," agrees his wife.

"I think you will too," he adds sharply. Even prophets are not
always compassionate.

"Perhaps we'll die at the same time," his wife suggests.

The husband contemplates this notion for a while. Sadly, his
meditation distracts him from his earthly duty of drying dishes,
and the drying process grinds to a halt.

"No," he says at last. "I don't think that will happen." He
does not explain his reasoning. Prophecies rarely come with
explanations.

"We might both turn into trees at the same time," proposes
his wife. "We might be suddenly changed into trees by a benev-
olent god."

"Or we might die of heart attacks. Lots of people die of heart
attacks these days."

"It isn't impossible to suddenly turn into a tree. It has been
known to happen."

"And there's always cancer. You'll probably die of cancer if
you don't die of a heart attack."

"What was the guy's name? The guy who got turned into a
tree with his wife?"

"You know, I think I'm going to get cancer *and* a heart attack.
I'll have cancer for a while and bam! Heart attack will get me."

"Philemon and Baucis."

"What?"

"Philemon and Baucis. Neither one wanted to die before the other, so some *god* turned them into trees."

"Into dead trees?"

"No, living trees."

"So they would still have to die of something. And one would probably die before the other. The *god* didn't really solve their problem." There is a pause. Such canny observations do not often originate from the husband.

"They were probably chain-sawed to pieces in a most painful manner," says the wife. "The *god* probably turned them into trees, and then took a chain saw to them for fun."

"I'll bet he didn't cut both of them down at once, either," says the husband. "I bet he cut down one, and then waited, and *then* cut down the other one."

"Probably," the wife agrees.

The son has entered the kitchen. He has advanced quietly, and only now do his parents become aware of him.

"Why don't you help us with the dishes?" his mother asks. The question is meant to be rhetorical.

"Because I'm allergic to water," the son replies. The father stops drying. He is contemplating his son's comment.

"Then why are you always taking showers?" demands his father triumphantly, returning to his drying.

"Because I am a masochist." The drying stops again. The mother, used to such contradictions, continues washing.

"Do you remember Egerdon Castle?" the son asks suddenly.

The parents are somewhat taken aback. Their son has always carried himself with a studied indifference toward all things, making his asking a question quite startling. "Not specifically," says his mother. "We saw some castles when we were in England."

"Why?" asks his father.

The son's interest in the matter is abruptly extinguished. "Nothing. I was just reading something . . . it mentioned Egerdon Castle."

The fact that the son has asked a question is a surprise to his parents. But the shock of knowing that this question stemmed from something he *read*: this is a blow that threatens to drive the father to the heart attack he has prophesied.

"What did you read?" his father shouts. A book with the ability to arouse interest in his son is surely a book possessing supernatural powers.

The son decides not to tell his parents. He is given to such arbitrary withholding of information, especially when it serves to annoy his father. Instead, he opts for a change of subject.

"Someone called just now. They wanted to know if either of you were home."

"I imagine you told them we weren't," says his mother.

"I didn't say one way or the other. But they didn't seem to want to talk to you. They just wanted to know if you were home."

"That could have been an important call!" shouts the father, bent on defeating his son in a battle of decibels.

"Should I call the person back and assure them that both of you are, indeed, safe and sound at home?"

The father has become enraged. His state of mind is having a happy effect upon the dishes, which he is drying furiously.

The phone rings. The father charges to the cordless on the table.

"What?" he yells into the receiver.

"Why can't anyone in your family just say hello?"

"What?"

"My father died today, and all you people do is torment me." The father is baffled. He remains silent.

"You were home all along, weren't you? You prick!" The father continues his silence. The caller hangs up.

It is then that the father receives the heart attack he has been expecting all evening.

The mother will say later that the evening's misfortunes were brought about by unhappy circumstance. The father, from his bed in the hospital, will blame his son. The son, who is immune to guilt, will blame his father's diet. But no one will think to blame the *god*, chain saw in hand, who has been biding his time for just such an opportunity.

EMMA DONOGHUE

What Remains

She hasn't asked for me in two months. I check with her nurses, though it's a little humiliating. "Has Miss Loring by any chance asked for me?" I say. Lightly, as if it doesn't matter either way.

That's what they call her: Miss Loring, or sometimes Frances. She's not Queenie to anyone but me.

I wheeled myself in to her room today. She was lying there like a whale ready for the axe. "Queenie," I said, "it's me. It's Florence." Which sounded absurd, as I've never had to tell her who I am before, she always knew. What a pass we've come to, if I need to introduce myself! Like that line in the Bible. *The people who walk in darkness.* Brains rot like fruit in the end. I don't pity her for going senile. It's worse being a witness.

I try to keep a grip on the numbers myself. The nurses start to worry if you get the numbers wrong. It's 1967 and I'm eighty-five years old. I should by rights be dead. Queenie's not even eighty. I ought to have gone first. It shouldn't be like this.

I always thought it would be all right so long as we ended up in the same place. She collapsed just before our final exhibition, and I fell sick a week later, and when we were both moved to this Home just north of Toronto, I thought, Well, at least we'll be together. No need to fuss with cooking or shovel our own snow anymore; we'll get to talk all day if we want.

But there's more than one kind of distance that can come between people. This is our third year here. Her door says Miss F. Loring, mine says Miss F. Wyle, and they might as well be a thousand miles apart, instead of a fifty-foot corridor. Since Queenie's last attack, her eyes barely move when I wheel into her room, and she doesn't seem to recognize my name.

What's important, I suppose, is for me to keep remembering. What matters is to hold on to what's left.

Each one must go alone down the dark valley.

I wrote that poem a long time ago, before I knew what I was talking about. My father used to say Man was the only creature capable of sleeping on his back, so that was how we should sleep. To mark the difference, you see; to show that we were a Higher Form. I did try; I started every night flat on my back but it hurt my bones and I couldn't breathe. My father would come to wake me in the morning and find me curled up on my side and shake me awake. "Florence," he'd roar, "you look like an animal!"

When I was six I found a rooster with a broken leg. I fixed him just fine, mostly because my father said I'd never manage it. It was animals that turned me towards art. I saw a bird, and then a picture of a bird, and it all came together. If I couldn't be a bird then at least I could make one. Once a cat of ours died, and I asked if God had taken her to heaven, and my father said there was no room for animals in heaven. That's the day I stopped believing in God. Rosa Bonheur the French sculptor believed in metempsychosis, which means that human souls migrate into animal forms. She lived with her friend and a whole ark of animals and painted them. I suppose it seemed to her that we're all just creatures in the end.

Mind you, I'd shoot a dog if it got as crazy as Queenie.

Sixty years this month since we met in that Clay Modelling class in Chicago. She was big and I was small. She was beautiful and I was not. Her family adored her and mine didn't care for me. She grew up in Geneva, Switzerland; I came from Waverly, Illinois. She thought she liked men and I thought I hated them.

She had faith in politics and I wrote poems about trees. She worked in spurts; I did a little every day. All we had in common was a taste for clay.

Today her hands lie on the sheet like withered bananas. I remember a time when they were swift and sure and tireless. Like the Skeena River in full flood, that time I went to the Indian village to model the old totem poles. When was that? Back in the twenties sometime? Damn it. Gone.

That's us these days, a couple of old totem poles. Tilting at mad angles, silvery as ash, fading into the forest.

At the Art Institute in Chicago, the Master used to pinch all us girls on the bottom. He called it the *droit de maître*. Queenie didn't much mind. I slapped his hand away and called him a damn fool. Later he spread a rumour we were a couple of Sapphists.

There was another thing Queenie used to say: You can't go through life worrying about what people think of you.

Some days she's got more of a grip than others. She still doesn't ask for me, but when I go in to her room she sometimes seems to know who I am.

I tell her uplifting stories.

"Remember Adelaide Johnson, Queenie?"

A flicker of the eyes.

"She was barely twenty when she fell down that elevator shaft in the Chicago Music Hall. Did it stop her?"

"Hell, no," says Queenie feebly.

I laugh out loud. "That's right. She won $15,000 in damages and went off to study her art in Europe!"

But Queenie's face is blank, like a block of marble that's never been touched by the chisel.

I will not feed my soul with sorrow, that was her favourite line in all my poems.

Some dates are so clear in my head it's as if they're chiselled there. We came to Toronto in 1913. Canada was a young country; there seemed infinite room. But we only really got established after the Great War. The towns needed so many memorials, they had to stoop to hiring women! Queenie used to say that her career was built on dead boys.

Sculptors, we called ourselves from the start. The word sculptress sets my teeth on edge. Work like ours called for sensible clothes. We took to trousers, as early as the twenties, plus men's shoes and baggy jackets.

I'm not allowed to wear my old grey flannels here. I suspect they've been thrown in the trash. Well, they were a little decrepit, I admit. Instead the nurses give me housecoats to put on, pink or orange: hideous. "Blue was my colour, Queenie, do you remember?" I usually wore a touch of pale blue.

Queenie was always the more bohemian dresser. At our studio parties she'd appear in purple velvet with a gold fringe, or a green satin cape. I told her once she looked like something out of the comic strips – the Caped Crusader, or the Emerald Evil – and she wasn't too pleased. There was always a trail of ash across her front because she was too busy talking to remember the ashtray.

They keep her clean and tidy here; that's another reason she doesn't look like herself. And you can't get hold of a cigarette for love nor money.

I am lost in this forest of days. I can't remember when I wrote that. I go through a sort of checklist of names in my head, in case I'm forgetting anything. Our dogs were Samson and Delilah. (Delilah tore our neighbour's fur coat, but it served her right for wearing such a thing.) We had two motor cars, first Susie, then Osgoode. (Queenie always drove, and never got any better at it; I read the maps.) Some of our sculptures were – are, I mean – *Dream within a Dream*, *Women War Workers*, *Torso*, *Girl with Fish*, *The Goal Keeper*, *Negro Woman*, *The Rites of Spring*, *Derelicts*, *Eskimo Mother and Child*, *The Miner*, *Sea and Shore*, *The Key*. There were others, I know there were others, but I can't recall their names just now. Some are sold, some are scattered, the rest are under dust-sheets in our cold locked-up studio in Toronto that was a derelict church until we moved in. I don't have any of them here, but I can see them more clearly than my own mother's face.

The thing about sculpture is, it's always a risk. It costs money to model it, cast it, carve it, even transport it. Clay's bad enough; bronze is terrible; marble's ruinous.

All this week Queenie's been yapping away in her head to old friends, dead or alive or who knows. Sometimes if I listen closely I can pick up hints of who it is. Yesterday I could tell it was A.Y. Jackson because she was thanking him for taking us out to dinner the day he sold his first picture. He and she seemed to be having a grand old time.

She always did like parties better than I did. We had forty-eight artists for Christmas, one year, as well as three beggars from the neighbourhood. Six turkeys got eaten down to the bone. In the evening there was chamber music, and I drank too much wine and was persuaded to show them all how to do an Illinois hog call.

"Remember Liz Prophet, Queenie?"

"Mm," she says, ambiguously.

"That awful gallery in Rhode Island, they said they had nothing against showing a black girl's sculptures so long as she promised not to come to the opening. Barbarians! Do you remember what she did, Queenie?"

Silence.

I fill in with barely a pause. "Ran away to gay Paree."

"That's right," whispers Queenie.

"That's right," I repeat. "Lived on tea and marmalade."

"Stole food from dogs."

This detail cheers me immensely. Her memory's still in there, like the shape locked inside the marble. "That's right, my dear, Liz Prophet had to steal food from Parisian dogs. What was it you used to say to me in our bad winters? No one's got a right to call herself an artist until she's starved a little!" Her eyes have gone unfocused, milky blue.

She still keeps that photograph on her bedside table, the one of Charlie Mulligan, who taught her marble cutting back in the 1900s.

"Isn't he a fine fellow?" she's taken to asking the nurses, sometimes four times a day. I bet she doesn't remember his name either.

"Was he your young man, Miss Loring?" one of them said this morning, to humour her.

"That's right."

"Was he the love of your life?"

"That's right, that's right," Queenie repeats in a whisper, like a child. "The love of my life."

She doesn't mean Charlie Mulligan, by the way. That wild German she nearly married back in 1914, he's the one she used to call the love of her life. Not that I know what that means. Which life is she talking about when she says stupid things like that? As far as I know, the life she had was the one she spent with me.

I will not feed my soul with sorrow,
Not while dark trees march in naked majesty
Across the sunset sky.

When I wrote that, ten years ago, we still had the farm: 150 acres of wild quince and poison ivy by the Rouge River. These days I have a room with a small window facing onto the parking lot. I haven't seen a tree in a while.

Queenie doesn't know anyone today. She's got butter on her double chin. A journalist once asked her, "Miss Loring, do you specialize in memorial sculpture because of a special sympathy for the dear departed?"

I had to cut in; I couldn't resist. "No," I said, "it's because she likes climbing ladders."

It was true. She's always liked to work on a grand scale. She's built on a grand scale too.

The local children used to call us the Clay Ladies. That was because we showed them how to make things out of clay, of course, but the phrase fitted us too, more and more as the decades went by. These days we look like works in progress, there's no point pretending otherwise. Queenie's a vast model for a monument – all two hundred pounds of her clay slapped onto a gigantic wire armature – and as for me, I'm some skinny leftover. Maybe I'm a Giacometti and she's a Henry Moore! Not that I'm a fan of the so-called moderns; most of them couldn't draw a human body if they tried, and as for beauty, I doubt they could even spell it. Boring holes in things! – that's not sculpture, that's vandalism.

To think she and I used to be something. A unit; a name. The Loring-Wyles.

I'm not saying it was all fun and games. We had a couple of bad years. We sometimes considered suicide, only half-joking. But we didn't think we should depart alone; we wanted to take at least a dozen enemies with us. On dark February evenings in the studio we amused ourselves by drawing up a list.

But if there's no heaven, what remains?

All this week Queenie's been having delusions. She sits up in bed, the sheets draped around her like snow on the Niagara Escarpment. She shakes her fists over her head and pants with effort. The nurses say if she doesn't calm down she's going to bring on another attack.

Finally today I figured out what she's doing. She thinks she's carving her lion, all over again.

"Why a lion?" I asked her, nearly thirty years ago.

She laughed. "Isn't it obvious, Florence? A snarling, defiant lion; rising from a crouch, ready for a fight."

Well, this was 1940.

It was to be a huge, stylized sort of lion, guarding the entrance to the new Queen Elizabeth Way near Toronto, to commemorate the visit of the King and Queen. I wouldn't have thought it was possible to do anything new with a lion, but Queenie's design was a wonder: the beast's face and ruff and whole muscled body were made up of great smooth arcs of stone.

It was just about the most gruelling project Queenie ever dragged us into, and that's saying something. I say we, but I was only doing a bas-relief of Their Majesties on the back of the column. Queenie's lion had to be carved on site, emerging from the column, as it were. She planned to use Indiana limestone – lovely flawless stuff – but no, word came down that for patriotic reasons it had to be Queenston limestone, which was twice as hard and pocked with holes. That was bad enough, but hiring a stone cutter was the worst. The top three men on our list were struck off by government order as "enemy aliens," even though the German had been reared in Canada and the Italians were the best in the trade. Instead, Queenie had to put up with a true-blue Englishman whose work she'd never trusted.

He couldn't take orders from a woman, that was his problem, and he wasn't the only one, let me tell you. We had to scour the country to find a cutting machine for the fellow, and he still didn't get started till August of that year. When we drove down in November to check his progress, the rough outlines of the lion had only half-emerged from the column. "The fellow hasn't even started on the hind quarters," muttered Queenie.

I thought the neck looked a little odd. Queenie asked him about it. "Oh, yes, actually, Miss Loring," said the fellow, evading her eyes, "I changed the line a little, to make it lie better."

The cheek of the man! I didn't blame her for firing him on the spot, even with all the horrors that followed.

Queenie couldn't find another qualified cutter in Canada. She consulted the union, who told her that only their members were permitted to cut stone for sculpture. She told the union to go to hell, she'd finish it herself.

Neither of us had ever used a cutting machine. The December winds howled in off the lake. I remember craning up at Queenie on the scaffold, which we'd swathed in tarpaulins as a feeble shelter. She was fifty-two that year, and already a huge woman. Her hands were swollen with arthritis.

"Queenie!"

"Don't you fret, Florence," she shouted down.

"It's not worth it," I bawled. "Give it up!"

She pretended not to hear. I could tell, from the way she handled the machine, that she was in pain. The planks of the scaffold buckled under her weight. Specks of snow fell on her head.

I cursed her, but the wind ate up my words. "What if you fall?" I screeched.

She peered over the tarpaulin, her face drawn but hilarious. "I'll probably bounce!"

She didn't fall. Next day she abandoned the machine and picked up her biggest chisel and hammer. If I'd been a praying sort of woman, I'd have prayed then. As it was, I stood and shivered and watched, week after week. I remember wondering what would happen to us all if Hitler won the war.

The snow held off just long enough. The lion crawled from his block, metamorphosing like something out of Ovid. By the time Queenie dropped her tools, her hands were like claws, but the lion was magnificent.

On his pedestal, in deep-cut letters, it said something about "the Empire's darkest hour" and this work having been done "in full confidence of victory and a lasting peace." I remember it because it was on the day of the Highway's official opening, as we stood below the lion with the lake wind lashing our scarves against our numb faces, that it occurred to me that I was a Canadian. Not that I'd ever got around to filling in the forms; on paper I was – as I am still – a U.S. citizen. But sometimes things about you change without you noticing.

So that's how the story ended. Only, for Queenie, I see now, it's not over. It's 1967 but she can't be convinced her war work is done. She still straddles the scaffolding, high above Lake Ontario. Her hands grip huge imaginary tools.

"Just another quarter-inch," she mumbles hoarsely.

"Lie down, now," I tell her. "Nurse says it's time for your sponge bath."

"In a minute," she says, austere. Her arm moves as if to hammer the air, and she speaks to me as if I'm a stranger. "I don't think you appreciate the urgency of my work."

"Of course I do," I murmur.

Then her head turns, and her blue eyes bore into mine, and her voice rises.

"It may have escaped your attention," she roars, "but there's a war going on!"

"But Queenie," I say for the hundredth time, "your lion's finished." She gives me a weary look, as if she sees through all my wiles.

"Everyone loves him! They say he's the finest monumental sculpture in Canada." Well, that's not quite a lie; some people did say that, once.

She shakes her head. "I still need to do his ears. And his back paws, and his tail."

"No, he's all done. I'll prove it," I say rashly. And then it occurs to me that I can.

I've struck a deal with the Home's handyman. But the Head Nurse says she'll have to speak to the authorities. "On the Queen Elizabeth Way, Miss Wyle?" she repeats, unconvinced.

"Just at the entrance."

"A lion?"

"You must have seen it," I tell her. "You couldn't miss it if you've ever driven down to Niagara."

And then it occurs to me that she thinks I'm the one who's gone gaga. Delusions of lions. "It's a stone lion," I clarify coldly. "You may not know that Miss Loring and I are sculptors. Our work is to be found in many cities and galleries across Canada."

"Yes," she says, as if placating me.

"Besides," I snap, "as far as I am aware we are voluntary residents here. If we choose to be taken on a drive by a kind young man on his afternoon off, I can't see that you have any right to object."

She butts in. "Miss Loring isn't strong –"

"My friend is well enough to sit in a motor car. It's her mind that's troubled. And what I propose to do will set her mind at rest."

I sound more sure than I am.

The air smells clean. The May sunshine dazzles me. I cover my eyes. A Bug, the young handyman calls it. Looks like a Henry Moore car to me; all bulges and holes. He lifts me out of my wheelchair and puts me in first, then I help to tug Queenie in through the other door. Occasionally she laughs. It takes us a quarter of an hour. I can tell the boy's surprised at my strength. My legs may be kaput but my skinny arms are still a sculptor's.

"Are you comfortable, Miss Loring?"

No answer from Queenie, who's examining one of her knees as if she's never seen it before. The boy gives me a doubtful glance.

"Yes, yes, she's fine, let's be off," I tell him. So he wheels our chairs back into the Home, then starts up the engine.

Toronto is a blur of sunlight and glass highrises. I glance idly into shop windows – bikinis, Muskoka chairs, sunflowers – not letting myself wonder if this is the last time I'll ever see the city.

We're at the Queen Elizabeth Way in less than an hour. The lake glitters like tinsel. Our driver looks over his shoulder. "Where do you want me to stop, Miss Wyle?"

"Just by the entrance."

"Oh. Only, I don't think it's legal. I mean, everyone else is going pretty fast."

"Let them," I say, autocratic. "Park on the verge."

"Couldn't I just slow down a bit as we go past this statue of yours?"

"No you could not. Pull over."

He wheels onto the shoulder and we come to a shuddering stop. "It's dangerous," he remarks. "What if the cops come by?"

"Tell them you've got two octogenarians having heart attacks in the back of your car."

That shuts him up. He turns off the engine. I roll down my window jerkily, and lean out, squinting into the sun.

"Look, Queenie, your lion!"

She keeps on staring into her lap. The boy sits with his arms folded, as if embarrassed by us. I lean over her bulk and tug at the handle till the dirty glass slides down.

"Go on," I say eagerly. "Put your head out and have a look. He's finished. He's splendid."

Finally she seems to hear me. She leans her head to one side, lolling out the window. Dust blows in her face as a chain of cars rushes by. I hang out the window on my side and stare at the stone beast, as good as new if a little darker. Nearly thirty years, and not a mark on him. He could stand there forever. There, I want to tell Queenie, that's what remains of us.

I reach over to take her hand. But she has her head down again; she seems to be examining an egg stain on her lapel. A dreadful thought occurs to me. I let go of her hand and wave my fingers in front of her face. She doesn't flinch.

"Queenie?"

She looks in my direction. Her eyes are calm and milky. She can't see a thing.

I should have guessed. I should have remembered her eyes were getting worse; I would have, if I'd half a brain left myself.

"What do you think of your lion now?" I ask her softly, just to be sure.

She says nothing for a minute, and then, "Lion?"

I don't answer her. After a minute I lean over to roll up her window. Then I tell the boy he can take us back to the Home now.

An enormous tiredness settles on me. I lay my head on the seat back at a peculiar angle. I shut my eyes to escape from the sunlight. *Each one must go alone down the dark valley.* I keep hold of Queenie's hand, but only because I can't think of anything else to do.

"Blue," she murmurs, half an hour later at a traffic light, and I don't know what she means: the lake? the sky? or just what she remembers of the colour that used to go by that name?

"That's right," I say, "blue."

Florence Wyle (1881–1968) and Frances Loring ("Queenie," 1887–1968), the "Loring-Wyles," remain two of the most important sculptors in the history of Canadian art. Born in Illinois and Idaho respectively, they met at the Chicago Art Institute in 1907, and spent almost sixty years working and living together, mostly in Toronto. After spending several years in a nursing home in Newmarket, Ontario, where they both gradually became senile, they died within three weeks of each other.

For this story I have used information from Rebecca Sisler's biography *The Girls* (1972), and have also drawn on some of Florence Wyle's published poems. But this fictional account of their declining years, and a trip to see the lion, is my own invention. Frances Loring's lion has been moved to parkland near its original site at the entrance to the Queen Elizabeth Way between Toronto and Niagara.

KAREN MUNRO

The Pool

This is the story of our lives. We type things up – novel manuscripts, advertising copy, annual reports, manifestos – and when we're done typing we stack them neatly on the floor and the cat moves from pile to pile, shredding. Several times a day we get up from our desks and use our whisks and dustpans to sweep up the debris. If it accumulates too much we might be reprimanded, and no one can afford to be reprimanded. We retype what the cat has shredded, we restack the papers carefully, we watch the cat from the corners of our eyes as it wanders around the room.

We don't talk. We are a typing pool, not a quilting bee; we aren't allowed to talk. Instead, one of us types a motion and places it on top of the stack on the desk of the woman next to her. That woman reads it and passes the message along, before the cat can shred the sheet. And so on down the line. In this manner we have run through almost every course of action we can imagine.

We have suggested taking out the cat – sometimes literally, as in putting it outside on the fire escape, and sometimes metaphorically, as in with a stick. We vetoed this plan early because the cat belongs to Melanie, our employer. She brings it every day in a pink plastic carrier, and feeds it powdered cream from the shaker by the coffee stand. Twenty-two pounds, she tells us proudly.

But taking it out is out of the question, because a temp once pushed it off her desk with a ruler, saying she was allergic, and

Melanie invited her back to the photocopy room to show her the staple option. None of us moved, not even when the screaming started. We aren't brave enough to take the cat out, although a fringe faction in the corner tried to convince us that we could put it through the shredder while Melanie is on her break, and tell her it was an accident, that its tail got caught. One fiery-eyed young woman passed a paper on which she volunteered to sacrifice the little finger of her left hand to the shredder, so that we could say we attempted rescue. But we aren't ready for such violent revolt. We are a typing pool, not a band of vigilantes. We are bland-mannered, fiftyish, red-knuckled, liverspotted, pale-eyed, irresolute. And we are sensibly afraid for our jobs.

Another group suggested that we stage a strike, and demand that the cat be removed from the room. This is marginally more plausible, although still completely out. Melanie has posted anti-union flyers all around the office, like campaign posters. They're stapled over the employee bulletin board, new ones twice a month. Sometimes they disappear after Melanie's gone home. They say: THIS IS NOT A UNION WORKPLACE. YOU WERE INFORMED OF THIS WHEN YOU WERE HIRED. ATTEMPTS TO UNIONIZE ARE PUNISHABLE BY DISMISSAL. It's true, we were informed. During all of our interviews, Melanie informed us. Unions are bringing this country to its knees, she said, crossing her shapely legs and lighting a cigarette. There has never been a union in United Office Systems Incorporated, and there never will be. The door swings both ways.

We all agreed to this, of course. We needed the work, to stand between our paleness and utter dissolution. We have children and underemployed husbands. We are unskilled and we know it. Furthermore, we have all signed the contract and for six to eight months that's that. No one in the history of the pool has organized a union, unless you count the Horowitz sisters, who do a list at the start of each week, and make everyone sign to clean the ladies' room.

No union. No taking the cat out. We have considered other options. Someone suggested we feign allergies. She can't fire us for allergies, they said. We'll get medical certification. (How would we get such a thing? we wondered. Apparently, some of the temps have worked in medical offices, and have good relations with interns.) She can't fire us for that.

The eldest of us read these idealistic suggestions with a nostalgia for our own youthful simplicity. We remember Blanche Lowenbrau, who two years ago missed a day for a hernia, and got her pink slip the next morning. Or Lois Flitch, who was never seen again after she took five days off for lupus. Melanie herself has never been sick, in all the years she has worked here. No unions and no sick days, is her policy.

What is left to us? Someone suggested going over Melanie's head to upper management. A cat in the workplace is unsanitary. We could complain about workplace conditions. It would be legitimate, a legitimate complaint.

The problem is this: upper management exists, but we don't know where. Mornings, we arrive at a quarter to nine; evenings, we leave at six o'clock. There is only Melanie and her twenty-two-pound cat to see us. We know there must be someone somewhere who takes an interest – who tabulates the annual reports, the input and output and cost efficiency – but we only see the stacks of paper and Melanie and the cat. We would gladly go over Melanie's head if we could, but there's nowhere for us to go.

We have run out of options. We are helpless. We need a champion. We need a plan. We pass papers back and forth, but no answers come from them. The cat has been here longer even than Ethel Bainbridge, sixty-one with a polyurethane hip and two daughters in jail. Melanie, or someone just like Melanie, has been here forever.

We are contemplating our oppression when Melanie enters, holding up a sheet of goldenrod paper. We notice warily that she is wearing fresh lipstick. When she has a new announcement to deliver she always puts on lipstick first. Employees will be limited to two five-minute toilet breaks daily, she tells us. If we have any comments, we are free to consult her; she will be at her desk for the next ten minutes.

For nine and a half minutes, nobody moves. Then Phyllis Goodbody, who has worked here for nineteen years and has a window desk, gets up. Phyllis is fifty-eight years old. She has legs like Italian sausage, thick and marbled. She has arthritis in her right hand and elbow, a husband with a glass eye from hunting snipe, an impotent son, no hope of grandchildren. We have typed with Phyllis Goodbody for nineteen years.

She walks through the rows of desks, and one by one we lift our heads and meet her eyes. Silently, we call out to her, saying *No, go back, sit down, type.* She looks at each of us as she goes by, affectionately and distantly, like a glamorous mother saying good night to her children.

We hear her whisper to Melanie. Melanie nods with sober attention. That's all. Phyllis walks back to her desk with the same tragic calm. We all know what will happen next, and it does. Melanie writes something out and puts it in an envelope, and at five o'clock the envelope is on Phyllis's desk. We don't see anyone put it there, but it's there. She picks it up and holds it carefully between her finger and thumb as she puts on her coat. No one says anything about it. On the way out we leave a circle of space around her, and even after we get down to the street, we don't speak. Phyllis walks away alone to her bus stop. Tomorrow she won't be here, we know.

And she's not.

From the moment we arrive, our typewriters are furious in conversation. The loss of Phyllis is an outrage. We can't stand for it. We won't. We will stage a revolt. We will form a union. If we have to burn the building we will do it. For once in our lives we will not fear the consequences of our actions. We will do what is right.

Melanie arrives late, and surprisingly, she seems to notice our unspoken rage. She releases the cat and walks to the centre of the room. Phyllis Goodbody has been transferred, she tells us, although nobody has asked. Out of concern for her health she has been moved to a less physically demanding department of United Office Systems Incorporated. She is very happy at the prospect of her new job. Melanie has just run into her in the elevator on her way up, and Phyllis sends us all her best. She tells us all to keep working hard, because United Office Systems Incorporated rewards its employees with highly considerate gradual retirement integration programs. She hopes that her example will inspire us to even greater effort on behalf of the company.

After Melanie finishes talking, there is a brief silence. Then we start typing again. Melanie makes a few rounds of the room, examining our stacks and pointing out mistakes, and then goes out to have a cigarette. As soon as she's gone we tear the papers from our machines, roll in fresh sheets, and start to type frantically to one another.

We ask each other what department Phyllis is supposed to have been transferred to; as far as we know there are no other departments. We wonder what could be less physically demanding than sitting and typing. The lie about Phyllis goading us to greater effort is particularly galling, because even the temps know she hated United Office Systems Incorporated. For thirteen years she typed contractions without apostrophes, so that the work would have to be redone at the company's expense. Gradual retirement integration programs my fanny, types Ethel Bainbridge. Phyllis is looking at the hard end of a deep-fry basket as we sit here.

The thought of this – Phyllis demoted to work even more disgraceful, even less remunerative, than what we do already – is appalling. Instead of galvanizing us, it withers our resolve. It reminds us that we are all dispensable. We can't afford to cross Melanie; we can't afford even to protest. The fury of our typing dies gradually, until at last we are back to doing our jobs. We pile our finished work in careful stacks on the floor, and the cat goes from stack to stack, shredding.

Melanie returns and telephones her fiancé. For forty-five minutes she discusses tulle and taffeta and blancmange. We type. No one asks to use the bathroom. The cat has a litter box against the wall by Melanie's desk, and it uses it twice, in full view of the room.

At eleven o'clock Melanie goes out for another cigarette. One by one we stop typing and sit with our hands on the keys. We look at the cat. It is lying on the floor by Melanie's desk, chewing on a sheet of advertising copy. For a couple of moments it is blithe; then, as the hate in the room solidifies, it looks up. The tip of its tail twitches once.

In another second we will break. We will leap from our chairs, all of us, and thirty shrieking women will bolt across the room wielding rulers and scissors and three-hole punches, to each take part in reducing the cat to paste, to jam, to a viscid hair-tufted smear not even Melanie could love. Our hands are turning to fists. Our legs are trembling beneath our desks. There are women here who have not climaxed in twenty years and more.

But the phone rings.

Not the phone on Melanie's desk, which rings often while she's out, and which we routinely ignore. The pay phone by the coat racks; the phone which is regularly left off the hook during working hours to prevent incoming calls for any of us. No one has thought to check it in years, but somehow it has been left in its cradle today, and it rings. At first we don't know what it is. We think it must be an alarm of some kind, set off by the sheer force of rebellion in the air.

Now we look at each other furtively, our fire gone. It's forbidden, of course, to talk on the phone. It's forbidden to leave our desks without permission. The cat stares around the room, its tail twitching.

At last Ethel Bainbridge gets up. We cringe at the scrape of her chair, but she stands and walks quickly between our desks to the phone. Our ears are alert for any sound of Melanie in the hall outside. Ethel picks up the phone. She says nothing, only listens. After a moment she hangs the phone up and walks back to her desk. She settles into her chair and begins typing. A moment later, the door opens and Melanie walks into the room.

She digs through her purse while we all type like madwomen, pretending never to have paused. The cat leaps to the top of Melanie's desk and rubs against her arm, but she pushes it away. There is at least some satisfaction in the sight. The cat can shred our work, it can mock us and bait us and take our portion as its own, but it can't inform on us. Melanie finds a pack of matches in her purse and goes out without a word. The cat sits uncertainly on the desk, stands up, walks a few paces, then sits again. Its ears are flattened.

Meanwhile, something has been circulating through the room. Its origin, we know without asking, is Ethel. Ethel and whoever was on the other end of the phone. A piece of paper is being passed from desk to desk; across it is typed only one word: WAIT. When it has made the rounds completely, the air in the room changes again. We have received a directive from a mysterious source. Somebody, somewhere, understands our situation. Somebody has a plan.

We all go back to work, typing manuscripts and manifestos, offering shy and encouraging smiles whenever our gazes meet. The cat grows calmer slowly, until at last it falls asleep where it is sitting. We listen to its little grunts and snores without malice; after a while we begin to type in time with them.

The next day we are all in place, typing without a word, when Melanie arrives at half-past nine. She senses something, some unaccountable difference in the air that has to do with our failure to be afraid. It's true: we are not afraid anymore. At home in our beds, alone or beside our sleeping husbands, bolstered by friendly solid unjudging pillows, we have dreamed of all kinds of release.

Melanie drops the cat carrier on her desk and walks twice around the room. No doubt she's hoping to find some contraband – a sticky bottle of liqueur smuggled in and shared, or a copy of *The Jimmy Hoffa Story*. There's nothing, of course, for her to find. Like Joan of Arc, we have angel voices guiding us. Nothing that she can take away.

Back at her desk, she lets the cat out, then drops the carrier to the floor with a crash. We go on typing serenely, as if she had never entered the room. We roll our finished pages gently free, place them on the stacks beside our desks, and turn to whatever is next. We have instinctively abandoned all our usual forms of sabotage; we are for once the well-oiled machine she has always wanted us to be.

For a few minutes she sits at her desk, flipping through papers but clearly not reading them, watching us from under her lids.

The cat stays close to her feet. She gets up to check the staff bulletin board, and when she sees that her anti-union posters are still hanging, she comes back with a crease in her brow. A few of us are smiling as we work; risky, but not overly so. If questioned we can always say we are thinking of a television program we saw the night before, or something we overheard on the bus this morning. She cannot pry deeply enough into us to see what is really going on.

And what is really going on? We are waiting, as we have been told to do. We are happy, because waiting is something we are good at. If we were not, we would not be here. We would be elsewhere, we would be in more prestigious and exciting lines of work, we would be *doing*. But we are here, for six to eight months at a stretch, and the stretches stretch out in a long, unforeseeable file until in retrospect they make up years and years, entire lifetimes, of waiting. For our children to grow up, for our husbands to be promoted or pensioned, for times to get better. For the impotent son and his wife to adopt. For the daughters to be paroled. For our lives to begin, or end.

Tell us to type and we do so sullenly, with ill grace. Tell us to wait and look again; we are already doing it. We've been at it since before we were born.

Melanie, on the other hand, grows impatient quickly. She checks her watch and drums her fingers and shuffles papers back and forth across her desk. She glares at us and at the cat. At last she reaches for her purse and takes out her cigarettes and matches. Without a word she gets up and leaves the room. When the door closes we all stop typing at once, and in the silence we hear her paused outside the door, listening. Our fingers hover over the keys, ready to start again if the doorknob turns. A moment more of waiting, and then her footsteps go quickly away down the hall. We sit back and turn our eyes to the cat.

The phone rings. Ethel gets up, and we all look to her. She lifts the phone on the second ring and says nothing, only listens. We can't see her expression because she faces the wall, but we see her nod once, then once more. She hangs up the phone and goes back to her desk. She starts to type, and after a moment of hesitation, we follow suit.

By the time Melanie comes back, we are all typing just as before, with swift economy and without mistakes. Covertly, we are circulating a message. This time the paper says, HAVE FAITH. We pass it from desk to desk with shaking hands. We feel as if we could float up from our seats and drift in intricate circles against the ceiling.

For the rest of the day nothing happens. In the evening when we go to put on our coats, we are still silent, but there is a change: we treat each other with greater care and kindness than ever before. The younger women help the older ones with their sleeves and scarves.

Melanie is there already when we come to work the next day. This is unusual; the only time she has ever arrived early was when her apartment was being fumigated. Clearly, she has been looking for evidence. And clearly, she has found nothing. We are not stupid enough to leave any evidence behind.

We file to our desks and sit down in silence. As one, we roll fresh paper into our typewriters; as one, we flip the platens onto the rolls. When we shuffle through our stacks, there is a sound like that of autumn leaves whirling on concrete. When we strike our first keys, we make a clatter like a company of horsemen in the streets.

Melanie sits rigid in her chair, her fingers squeezing the corner of her desk. The cat crouches beside her. Is it our imagination, or is the cat a little thinner today? Melanie has been neglecting its diet of powdered cream; she has been too busy watching us, and trying to stem our revolt.

Our typewriter bells jangle as one. We slam the carriages back with a crash.

The air in the room seems light and concentrated, and our every movement feels guided. None of us has ever been abroad, but if we had we might think of some of the great cathedrals of Europe, or Bernini's *Saint Teresa*, or even of the music of Wagner or Tchaikovsky. Instead, we find our thoughts turning to our girlhoods; to our first loves and innocent early wishes, and to the blue and open sky that seemed, in those days, to reach right around the world.

The stacks of finished work grow higher beside our desks. Melanie squirms and wriggles in her seat; at last she springs up, as if prodded from behind, and goes walking quickly around the room. When she peers over our shoulders we can smell the taint of sweat and fear she carries, and the odour transports us like incense.

She is just passing Ethel's desk when she looks over and sees the pay phone resting in its cradle. Her eyes widen, her mouth falls open – and then she is running, *running*, to the phone. She grabs the receiver in both hands, puts one heel high against the wall, and yanks. For a moment she makes no progress, and we are treated to a bizarre tableau: Melanie, her face plum-coloured, her lips drawn back from clenched teeth, a pale run unzippering the stocking of her planted leg. Then there is a deep wrenching sound and the steel cord pulls free from the box. Melanie staggers backward. We have all stopped typing, and the silence is awful.

We are waiting for her to say something, perhaps even to scream. Her lips have bled almost white and the rest of her face is red. There is sweat on her forehead and under the arms of her blouse.

She says nothing. She looks around at us – we are pale with shock – and smiles. She straightens her blouse and runs her hand over her hair. Then she walks back to her desk, opens her top right-hand drawer, and drops the receiver into it. She shuts the drawer with a bang.

Out of sheer habit we all turn back to our machines. We begin to type. Almost immediately someone makes a mistake, and the ratcheting of her roll as she pulls the paper loose is like the sound of tumblers turning in a lock. The air feels insubstantial again; it smells of must and inky ribbons, and of the weary floral perfumes of old women.

Melanie takes her cigarettes and matches from her purse and goes out without a word. The cat leaps down from her desk, seizes hold of a paper and starts to tear. We stop typing and watch it in silence, feeling its teeth in our hearts.

The days that follow are dark. We come to work alone or in small groups, no more than two or three of us who have met by chance on the sidewalk outside. We are pale and dull-looking, even to each other. Without asking, we know that none of us has slept well; that we have been short with our husbands and children; that we have stood at the sink or stove for half an hour at a stretch, holding some forgotten item and staring into space. We know we have all dreamed of breakage and despair. We see the moons beneath one another's eyes and know better than to ask.

Melanie, on the other hand, is radiant. She comes to work late, with high colour in her cheeks and a glitter in her eyes. She settles into her chair with an audible sigh of contentment; she dials her phone with a girlish glee. For hours, she engages in playful dispute with the fiancé – will the bridesmaids wear lemon taffeta or peach chiffon? Will the band play "Dixie Rose" or "I Feel Pretty"? When she goes outside to smoke, her heels make a happy tippy-tap as long as we can hear them. While she is gone, we put our hands in our laps, bow our heads, and settle into a leaden silence. This is the only small rebellion we will ever have.

All except one of us, that is. While Melanie is gone, one typewriter keeps typing, evenly and without mistakes, as if nothing had ever gone wrong in the world. Ethel sits with her back straight and her chin raised, peering through the bottoms of her bifocals at the papers she is copying. She doesn't look at any of us, but we all sneak glances at her from time to time. We don't understand her calm; we tell ourselves that she is an old woman, and she must be in shock. She can't have realized yet that we have lost. We pity her; we even fear for her. A woman Ethel's age does not adjust easily to total disappointment.

Strangely, Ethel's is the only stack of paper that the cat does not molest.

Days go by. We lose track of them, and of ourselves, until we are once more what we have always been – a pool. Occasionally during the day we lift our eyes to the phone, and the stump of wire on the box reminds us of our place in life. Wait, we were told. We are waiting still. Have faith, we were told. Faith in what? Our souls have been yanked from their sockets, and only the wiry stumps remain.

Melanie arrives one day with a sheaf of coloured papers in her hand. Smiling, she goes to the centre of the room and gestures for our attention. First, she says, she regrets to inform us that due to international competition, the domestic recession, and fiscal restraint overall, our wages are being cut. Second, an innovation in middle management requires that everything we now copy once must be copied twice, retroactive to the start of the year. Third, the company policy of six- to eight-month typist contracts has been revised; contracts will now be available only for six to eight weeks, with mandatory employee reviews preceding renewal. Last, the company's enforced retirement age has been rolled back to fifty-eight. All employees senior to this age will be offered United Office System's gradual retirement integration package, effective the end of the working day. She smiles at each of us, but at Ethel most of all.

What is there to say? We can't even claim to be very much shocked by the news – sooner or later, we expected to be punished.

Melanie goes back to her desk and sits. She riffles the sheaf of papers with a loving hand, and slowly we begin to type again. We don't look at Ethel. From the corners of our eyes we can see her; her back is still straight, her chin is still raised. But none of us can bring ourselves to look at her directly.

As the news settles in we begin to consider the conditions we have worked under for years; the silence, the surveillance, the petty wages and distrust. None of it seems so bad. If the cat demolished our handiwork, if we were forced to sweep up piles of our own hard hours of labour, what of it? We weren't creating anything of value, after all. Only sheets and sheets of words without meaning, sabotaged already in a hundred subtle ways. And the rule of silence – did it matter? We found other ways to speak. At least we were paid a wage we could live on. At least we had six to eight months of security, and the eldest of us had jobs nobody else would give us. Now we have nothing.

We are sorry now that we ever thought of rebellion. We wonder if there is any way to make amends; could we go to Melanie, singly or as a group, and say to her *We never meant . . . We never thought . . . We never wanted . . .*

Some of the temps have begun to cry.

We are too caught up in our misery to notice when a message begins to circulate. Or maybe there is no circulation; maybe the paper appears simultaneously on everyone's desk at once, its three bold words typed all in capitals, in the very centre of the page: DID YOU THINK. We see it, we read it, but we don't understand what it means. Did we think? We bury the paper hastily in our stacks, fearful that Melanie will see it and punish us further. We go on typing, wiping our noses surreptitiously on our sleeves.

But another paper appears, coughed up somehow from the piles on our desks. THAT YOU WERE. This gives us pause. We can see now that a sentence is being formed. But what will be its end? Did we think that we were . . . what? Worthy? Intelligent? Beautiful? Is this some hideous plan of Melanie's – has she turned our own ruse against us? Or will it say *forgotten, forsaken, cast out*? Is it the voice of our champion?

For a long time there is nothing – only the sound of our machines and the crunch of the cat's jaws on paper. And beneath that, perhaps, another noise. Something tidal, indefinite, distant. Melanie files her nails and glances in her pocket mirror. Her face is unconcerned. The noise seems to be growing, but maybe it's old ears, wishful thinking; she doesn't seem to hear anything.

We have fallen unconsciously into rhythm again; we are typing at a great speed and as one. Together, we reach the end of a line and our typewriters jangle their bells. Together, we crash the carriages back, and turn to the next page of work. And there on the top of our stacks is a single sheet, bearing a single word. The moment we see it, we know what to believe. It simply says: ALONE?

Without an instant of conference, we all set to typing the word, over and over again. We fill half a sheet in a matter of seconds, our carriages rocketing back and forth, our bells a cathedral. There is no other way we can think to express our joy. At last, Melanie looks up from her mirror; she has realized something is wrong. She half-stands, and opens her mouth to speak.

What happens next is something we cannot explain.

The phone rings.

At first, Melanie reaches for the receiver on her desk – she's already barking into it when she realizes it's the wrong one. She stands holding the receiver, staring at it dumbly, while we type at a mad gallop. Another ring. Melanie throws the desk phone down and stands staring at her upper right-hand drawer. The phone rings again. Melanie jerks open her drawer and pulls out the pay phone receiver. Her face is ashen. She holds the receiver at arm's-length, the cord hanging down like a snake.

Answer it! somebody yells. The distant sound is growing louder; we are sure of it. Melanie hesitates a moment longer, then puts the phone to her ear. She says nothing, but her face grows even paler as she listens. The keys of our typewriters are growing hot; is there smoke spooling out of their works? Melanie sits down suddenly in her chair, as if her legs have been kicked from under her. She stares fixedly ahead, the phone cord coiled in her lap.

There is a sudden hacking sound from somewhere in the corner of the room, and all our eyes turn to it. The cat is hunched on a heap of papers, its head low and its shoulders up. From its mouth protrudes a crumpled leaflet, stained with carbon. It shudders and gasps. *Down the hatch!* someone shouts. The cat's eyes are glazing over; its struggles are growing weaker. When it collapses we send up a cry of glee. We type even faster, our fingers blurring.

The noise we have been hearing is no longer distant; it is enormous, it is the roar of a great throng of people outside in the street. If we go to the windows we will see them, a brilliant endless flood of people. Our husbands may be out there, our sons and daughters, the children they will adopt. We hear shouting and singing; we hear our names called out.

Someone yanks her paper from the roll and the entire carriage of her typewriter wrenches free. She whoops and knocks it to the floor. It is only the first to go; in moments, typewriters all over the room are giving up the ghost. Metal springs and sprockets are popping out of every one, smoke is curling to the ceiling, broken keys are clattering to the floor. We pull our papers out and hurl them in the air. ALONE? ALONE? ALONE?

spirals down around us, like the joy and admiration of a crowd.

When we go to get our coats, Melanie is still sitting at her desk, clutching the phone and staring straight ahead. We cover the cat in drifts of paper – the best we can do for a burial – but for her we can do nothing. We form a loose circle about her desk, and stand for a moment in silence. Ethel lays three sheets of paper down in front of her. DID YOU THINK/THAT YOU WERE/ALONE? Then we wrap our scarves around our heads and go out in a single company, to join the celebration in the streets.

JONATHAN GOLDSTEIN

You Are a Spaceman With Your Head Under the Bathroom Stall Door

spaceman

There was a spaceman that he had met when he was a kid. In the war, Richie went through this period where he thought about him all the time.

"I don't know if you can hear me," he said late one night, "but what does all this look like from up there?"

his head under the stall door

"I *am* looking," Arthur said, "but I ain't laughing."

"I ain't laughing," he kept saying. His face was very serious.

Joanie's journal entries: grade 7

My nerves all started in grade six, around the time Pinkie locked me in my locker. After that it got hard to look at lockers in the same way, once I knew how dark they got with the door closed and how bad my mother's sandwiches made them smell in the end.

Today I had gym and I know that one of these days I'm going to slip on that stupid beam and crack my whole crotch open like a walnut. Mrs. Tessler's whistle goes through me like a wet cold and makes me feel like I'm actually *inside* a whistle.

Lenny, who's totally retarded and failed six grades and has a full beard, brought one of the girls into the boys' locker room. She said she kept her eyes closed the whole time which I think is a pretty dorky thing to do. Come on!

Mrs. Sternfeldt knocks Chachi's desk over almost every single day. She scatters his stuff all over the floor with the tip of her loafer. It's like the whole world is made of dog shit except for her and that loafer. She leafs through his reader and claims she can tell exactly what he had for dinner each night just by looking at the condiment smudged into the page. Yellow means he had hot dogs on the night of Monday's assignment. Knowing that I had hot dogs with my family on a Monday night strikes me as a very creepy thing for a teacher to know.

Dear Arthur,

Thank you so much for being such a big asshole and yes, you are good-looking, but so was Hitler to some people. You are my brother Richie's best friend but you are still mean and stupid and one day you will find yourself alone and you will then know what it feels like to feel like crap. I sincerely hope that you have a good life, because I can never be happy. You are a jerk and you and Pinky deserve each other. I understand her father owns some big factory and I am sure that if you play your cards right, you will one day have people around to treat like shit, but then you will still die a miserable jerk.

The best lunch I ever brought was this one time my mother forgot to buy bread and she gave me crackers and cheese. Don't ask me why this was so great.

domino

When Richie got back from the war he was missing a leg. They had a big party for him and some people even said he was a hero.

"There are no heroes in war," Richie said.

At the party he got up on stage and sang with his old band. In the middle of a Fats Domino tune, he fell down on the floor. When they tried to help him up, he shrieked: "Don't you ever manhandle a casualty, soldier."

Now he lived with his parents. He spent most of his time masturbating in his room. On the rare occasion that he went out, it was usually to pick up a copy of his favourite magazine. There were pictures of women tied to coffee tables and men using them as coasters.

Richie sat on the edge of his bed. He went at it slowly. He didn't want the springs to give him away.

three cute librarians

When Lenny and Andrew tried to gross each other out, Lenny would talk about the day he found Andrew's mother raking leaves in the backyard in her underwear and how cute her little waddle was.

Andrew talked about Lenny's aunt Betty. She had a mole on her cheek the size of a grapefruit and he'd go on about how wild she'd get when he'd gnaw on it. "I once bought her a nipple tassel for it and taught her to spin it clockwise *and* counter-clockwise. She's a talented old bird."

The day they started kicking each other's asses in front of the library was plenty ugly, the windows shaking, the librarians running outside screaming their heads off.

"I'll stick a bug so far up your ass," Andrew said as three cute little librarians tore Lenny's head out from under his armpit.

In Lenny's parents' basement, they started inventing their own language: "orange julep" was "unslep"; "french fries" was "enchify"; "hot dog" was "otenhog." They only got three words into the whole thing.

Sometimes they would lie in the basement at night and talk about what they would do if they were downtown.

"I'd go up to some girl," Andrew said, "and I'd make her love me."

"What if all of this is a dream?" Lenny said.

"I'm pretty sure it isn't," Andrew said.

antennae

Chachi told her he wanted to eat her ass. Joanie laughed and he said don't laugh because I'm dead serious. He leaned her against the wall and pulled down her pants. He had never eaten an ass before and didn't know where to start.

Joanie ordered a half a grapefruit and cottage cheese and he ordered soft-boiled eggs.

"I ought to have my head read," Chachi said. "If they don't bring me one of those little egg cups to put them in, do you know what a pain in the ass I'm in for? There's a trick for getting the shell off but I'll be damned if I can remember it."

"Will you relax?" she said.

"It's probably not too late to catch the waitress."

The room they moved into was already furnished. The left end of the coffee table was broken so it looked like a ramp. Chachi put his feet up anyway.

"The thing about coffee tables," he said, "is that they make you feel like you're a part of society."

After several weeks, it was starting to look like a dog with its head cut off. Underneath the overflowing ashtray was one of Joanie's nylons. There was a Superman comic under a bicycle lock.

"Do you still love me?" he asked.

She was examining the remote control when she noticed a button she had never seen before. It was orange and when she pressed it, everything in the room got very dark and quiet.

Chachi refused to wear a white shirt with the suit.

"Light blue is very in these days," he said.

At the wedding, Joanie kept telling him that they should dance. She was worried her family wouldn't think she was normal.

"This sherbet tastes like aftershave," Chachi said to the little boy seated beside him.

Everyone did this dance move. They did it in unison like the Solid Gold dancers. Chachi danced like he was trying to catch a glass of tomato juice that was falling off the fridge.

Joanie talked to her aunt who sat in a chair the whole night.

"If I could do it again," her aunt said, "I wouldn't be such a hot shot."

"Well, I had a perfectly lovely time," he said as they drove home.

"She has braces, for God's sake," she said.

Her hands were balled up into the tiniest fists. He could have fit the two of them in his mouth.

He put his hand on her knee and said: "When I was twelve, I jerked off every night thinking about you."

In her head she was trying to count how many cars she had ever driven. She got to eight when the car radio started to play, "Shaddapayou face."

"Whatsamatta you," they sang in unison.

Chachi dreamt that night that his mother was alive. They were fighting in the street.

"I have no more room in the house for toilet paper," he screamed.

"To make me happy," she said.

She was saving the Miami Beach ashtrays. The phone was ringing. He couldn't find paper towels. She showed up and it was pissing outside.

"I was happy to be left alone," he said.

"I was saving those," she cried. "I've been saving those since I was a little girl."

At the end of the night in the park, Joanie told him she wasn't nipping from the bottle at all. Every time Chachi passed it to her she only pretended.

This was the way she was and now he was twice as drunk as he should have been.

Arthur drives a cab

Arthur used to have thick long hair. Richie would brush it up and out until his head looked like a pompom. Richie said it was the latest style. He called it "The Beethoven."

Now Arthur was bald with a small scar on his forehead. He drove a cab and when he said "but um," he pronounced the "t" very hard.

Arthur told Richie about the woman from the night before who got into his taxi with an open umbrella. She had milky, pale blue eyes and when he took a fast corner, he heard her head hit the door and her eyes in the rear-view mirror didn't blink.

"The inside of my cab still smells like shepherd's pie."

heart attack

Lenny and Andrew still got together once in a while.

"There must be something," said Andrew.

"Believe me. I ask," said Lenny.

They would drink and talk about who they would rather do.

"Shirley," said Andrew.

"Laverne," said Lenny.

They drank more. Inevitably, they ended up in their underwear running around Lenny's mother's coffee table trying to tickle each other.

Once, when they had drunk too much, they played hide 'n' seek. At the end of the night, Andrew was in the trunk of the car in the garage, sleeping.

The next morning, in the parking lot at the Piggly Wiggly putting away the groceries, Andrew's mother had a heart attack.

Wisdoms: Richie's unfinished book

I never met a Tim or Timmy who wasn't a rat. Now that I tell you this, if you decide to go and name your son Timmy anyhow, then sir, you are a jerk.

To have lived a full life means to die happy.

Saturday night

"Remember," Chachi said, "it is I who is eating you. It is I who makes you feel pleasure."

Joanie was lying back thinking about Arthur. He was pumping her on the back of his motorcycle in the middle of a circle of screaming frat boys. There was an exchange of money and she would wake up the next morning on a lawn chair wearing Ray-Ban sunglasses.

"Who's your daddy," demanded Chachi.

cool

"I'm smacking and I'm smacking," said Arthur. "Christ! What a schmuck I am."

"Maybe Carmine's right." said Pinkie. "Maybe you're just losing your cool. That isn't so bad."

"Shut your fucking mouth," said Arthur.

He kept hitting the jukebox. Sometimes he would hit lightly and sometimes he would hit so hard, the chandelier would shake. Sometimes he would say "hey" and sometimes he would say nothing. He looked like he was going to cry.

Arthur peeled a motorcycle magazine off the coffee table.

"I'll be in my office," he said.

Right beside the jukebox, Pinkie did the twist.

goojoo

Richie's dad used to call mucus "goojoo." It was dripping out of him like he was a cracked egg about to lose his yolk.

"I love you, I love you," Richie kept saying.

hardware

Richie's dad owned a hardware store. Arthur walked in looking like he hadn't slept in days and had been chomping bennies by the fistful.

"Hey, Arty," said Richie's dad, "what can I do you for?"

"Mr. C., I need a wrench. I need to borrow a wrench."

"Are you all right?"

"No I'm not fucking all right." He looked like he was a half a second away from crying.

"Do you want a big wrench or a small wrench?"

"Fucking surprise me." Something sprayed out of his nose. He turned around and stared out the window with his arms crossed in front of him.

Mr. C. came back and tapped Arthur on the shoulder with a medium-sized wrench.

"Here you go," said Mr. C.

Outside, Arthur snapped his sunglasses out of his pocket. "First I'm going to twist his nipples off," he said.

The Big Ragoo

Carmine showed up at her house because he just happened to be in the neighbourhood. He just so happened to be wandering around in Pinkie's neck of the woods.

As he was climbing the stairs to her apartment he had this funny idea. He was going to knock really hard on her door and when she asked who it was he was going to say, "It's the Big Ragoo!" He was going to say it like a real New York Italian tough guy who ate cow's balls and salami for breakfast.

He faced her door and put one hand in his windbreaker pocket to get all into it. It's the Big Ragoo, he kept saying to himself.

He had never banged on a door that hard in his life. All the dogs in the apartment next door started barking. A man in shorts and beach tongs opened his door. The smell of Campbell's soup flooded the hallway.

Carmine faced Pinkie's door and inside he heard the jukebox. He waited for the squeak of her wooden floorboards to grow louder.

Thermos

Chachi imagined Joanie being smacked in the face when she was a little girl. She went to this terrible day care where they never let her change out of her wet bathing suit. Her mother sent her there each day with just a Thermos full of coffee. He imagined her tap dancing around the play mat for all the boys, never seeing the fat woman in the black polyester pants who wanted to set her straight. She was dancing like how she did at home on the kitchen table. The fat woman had a hand full of slaps for her since the day she first saw her.

The way Joanie found green glass so pretty, even if it was broken, hurt his heart.

"I told you I was making the place more cozy," she said.

Her feet smelled like his childhood.

carnival

The girl selling kisses was named Peggy. She had red frizzy hair. There was something about her that made Richie think of orange juice in a greasy glass and leftover ketchup but she was selling kisses and he was hard up.

Her booth was right beside the haunted house. She was busy applying lip-gloss as he pulled out a crumpled ball from his pocket. He flattened it against his leg into a nice respectable dollar bill.

"That was magical," she said afterwards.

"Sure," he said.

"No really," she said.

"No really," he said.

new year's

There was six of them: Joanie and Chachi; Lenny and Andrew; and Richie and Peggy. They sat on bridge chairs in a circle. Joanie brought out a bottle of champagne and one of the men popped it and then no one had anything to say. Joanie started to cry as a joke.

flappers

Richie liked looking at naked flappers. These women were all dead but their spirit lived on in his erection and when he came they died all over again.

nobody, not even Joe Pesci, has such small hands

"I didn't say you were a fucking idiot," Chachi said. "I said you were *like* a fucking idiot."

Joanie was cleaning out the room of all her things. She was a methodical Zamboni.

After she left, he saw a shimmering ring of celestial light in the middle of the double parlour and when he stepped through it, he was in the bathroom of his childhood house. He was crying on the floor, pulling toilet paper off the spool with both hands like he was climbing a rope.

sauce

For eight years, Richie never felt like himself. When he woke up in the morning, his stomach felt like a sandwich bag full of Sea Monkeys.

There would come a time after his mother's death when he would have to clean out the big freezer in the basement. Inside he would find ice-cream containers filled with blocks of spaghetti sauce. He could eat those for a while and think: *Pretty soon I will never be able to eat her sauce again.*

Joanie's journal entries: grade 12

I once loved this guy so much I didn't care what made sense. I bit his nose until he cried and even then I couldn't stop.

My mother wanted to talk with me. "I found this in your coat," she said. I rolled over, my face to the wall. "Oh, Mom, I love you. I don't want you to die."

"Why can't you ever be serious," she said.

It was night and it was raining so hard that something felt spiteful. It was like breathing underwater. I stopped in front of three men standing under a fruit store awning. They checked me out. I was wearing black jeans and I looked at them and just peed and peed.

They never could have known.

God

Richie woke up in the middle of the night and felt nothing but that he was alive. This was the panic he kept trying to describe. *Being*.

"Cripes, Eddy," he would say to God, "I'm really over a barrel here."

Chachi's notes towards a telephone conversation with Joanie

– glad you caught her
– sounding effervescent as always (joke)
– how was your summer

only if things are going well:

– I think about you a lot – the stuff about the little girl on the boardwalk, candy apple, bag of cheesies
– just want to see your face – miss seeing it
– you were the best thing that ever happened to me.

Kojak

Richie shaved his head and walked into the bakery he always went to.

"Hey, Kojak," said the Chinese woman who worked there and like usual, he ordered one sugar doughnut.

Outside the window, it was raining. He saw a girl walk by in a dress of paper towels.

About the Authors

Mike Barnes is the author of *Aquarium* (The Porcupine's Quill), which won the 1999 Danuta Gleed Award for best first collection of stories in English. His poetry collection, *Calm Jazz Sea* (Brick Books), was shortlisted for the Gerald Lampert Memorial Award. His stories have appeared twice before in *The Journey Prize Anthology* (volumes 11 and 13), and in *99:Best Canadian Stories*. His first novel, *The Syllabus*, will be published by The Porcupine's Quill in October 2002. "Cogagwee" will appear in his second collection of stories, to be published by The Porcupine's Quill in spring 2003.

Geoffrey Brown lives in Ottawa. He is the author of the novel *Notice* (Gutter Press).

Jocelyn Brown lives in Edmonton. Her first book, *One Good Outfit*, was published by Mercury Press in 2000. She is currently working on *Mistakes & Improvements*, a novella and short story collection. "Miss Canada" was also nominated for a National Magazine Award.

Emma Donoghue was born in Ireland in 1969 and now lives in London, Ontario. Her novels include *Stirfry*, *Hood*, *Kissing the Witch*, and *Slammerkin*, which was shortlisted for the Irish Times Fiction Prize. Her latest book is a collection of short stories, *The Woman Who Gave Birth to Rabbits*. For more information, check out www.emmadonoghue.com

Jonathan Goldstein is a native of Montreal. He is currently living in Chicago, where he is a producer at public radio's Peabody Award–winning *This American Life*. He was the host of CBC Radio's *Road Dot Trip*. His first novel, *Lenny Bruce Is Dead* (Coach House Books), received the 2002 ReLit Award.

Robert McGill was born on Ontario's Bruce Peninsula and until recently has lived in England, where he published short fiction in *Paper, Scissors, Stone* and *The May Anthologies*. "Confidence Men" and "The Stars Are Falling" are his first short stories to appear in Canadian journals. He now lives in Toronto, where he is working on a novel.

Nick Melling was born in Victoria and currently attends the University of British Columbia. "Philemon" was written during his high-school creative writing class and is his first published story.

Robert Mullen is an American-born naturalized Canadian presently residing in Edinburgh, Scotland, with his British-born wife. His short fiction has appeared in North America, the United Kingdom, and Spain. He has published a short story collection, *Americas*, and has recently completed a second collection as well as a novel. "Alex the God" comes out of an interest in ancient history and a year spent living in Lebanon.

Karen Munro graduated from the Iowa Writers' Workshop in 1999. She lives in Vancouver, British Columbia, where she works as a librarian.

Leah Postman holds an M.F.A. degree in Creative Writing from the University of British Columbia, and is currently at work on a book of linked short stories. "Being Famous" is her first published short story; it was also shortlisted for a Western Magazine Award. She lives in Vancouver with her husband and two small daughters.

Neil Smith is a translator and writer from Montreal. Recently, he has adapted a French children's song about the Woman in the Moon and translated a museum exhibit on the wacky mating rituals of animals and insects. His short stories have appeared in *Event*, *Blood and Aphorisms*, *The Antigonish Review*, and *Headlight*. "Green Fluorescent Protein" was inspired by a Brazilian artist who created a glow-in-the-dark bunny.

About the Contributing Journals

For more information about all the journals that submitted stories to this year's anthology, please consult *The Journey Prize Anthology* Web site: www.mcclelland.com/jpa

Broken Pencil is the magazine of zine culture and the independent arts. We review underground publications, including zines, indie-published books, videos, artworks, e-zines, and music. We run groundbreaking features on art, culture, and society from an independent perspective. We reprint from the best of the underground press. In each issue, the new fiction section of the magazine celebrates the edgy and the unpredictable. For a sample copy please send a $5 cheque or concealed cash to *Broken Pencil*. Submissions and correspondence: *Broken Pencil*, attention Fiction Editor, P.O. Box 203, Station P, Toronto, Ontario, M5S 2S7. Web site: www.brokenpencil.com

The Claremont Review is Canada's international literary journal showcasing the work of young adult writers, aged thirteen to nineteen. We have published the best in poetry, fiction, short plays, and graphic art for ten years, in the spring and in the fall. We sponsor an annual poetry contest, with a deadline of March 15. All submissions accompanied by an S.A.S.E. will receive a handwritten comment. We do not read in July and August. Submissions and correspondence: *The Claremont Review*, 4980 Wesley Road, Victoria, British Columbia, V8Y 1Y9. Web site: www.theclaremontreview.com

Descant is a quarterly journal, now in its third decade, publishing poetry, prose, fiction, interviews, travel pieces, letters, literary criticism, and visual art by new and established contemporary writers and artists from Canada and around the world. Editor: Karen Mulhallen. Managing Editor: Mary Newberry. Submissions and correspondence: *Descant*, P.O. Box 314,

Station P, Toronto, Ontario, M5S 2S8. E-mail: descant@web.net
Web site: www.descant.on.ca

Event, established in 1971, is published three times a year by
Douglas College in New Westminster, B.C. It focuses on fiction,
poetry, creative non-fiction, and reviews by new and established writers, and every spring it runs a creative non-fiction
contest. *Event* has won regional, national, and international
awards for its writers. Editor: Cathy Stonehouse. Assistant
Editor: Ian Cockfield. Fiction Editor: Christine Dewar.
Submissions and correspondence: *Event*, P.O. Box 2503, New
Westminster, British Columbia, V3L 5B2. E-mail (queries only):
event@douglas.bc.ca Web site: event.douglas.bc.ca

Exile is a quarterly magazine which features Canadian fiction
and poetry as well as the work of writers in translation from all
over the world; some the best known, others unknown.
Publisher and Editor: Barry Callaghan. Submissions and correspondence: *Exile*, P.O. Box 67, Station B, Toronto, Ontario,
M5T 2C0.

The Fiddlehead, Canada's longest-running literary journal, publishes poetry and short fiction as well as book reviews. It appears
four times a year, sponsors a contest for poetry and fiction with
two $1,000 prizes, including the Ralph Gustafson Poetry Prize,
and welcomes all good writing in English, from anywhere,
looking always for that element of freshness and surprise.
Editor: Ross Leckie. Managing Editor: Sabine Campbell.
Submissions and correspondence: *The Fiddlehead*, Campus
House, 11 Garland Court, P.O. Box 4400, Fredericton, New
Brunswick, E3B 5A3. E-mail (queries only): fid@nbnet.nb.ca
Web site: www.lib.unb.ca/Texts/Fiddlehead

Grain magazine provides readers with fine, fresh writing by new
and established writers of poetry and prose four times a year.
Published by the Saskatchewan Writers Guild, *Grain* has earned
national and international recognition for its distinctive literary

content. Editor: Elizabeth Philips. Fiction Editor: Marlis Wesseler. Poetry Editor: Seàn Virgo. Submissions and correspondence: *Grain*, P.O. Box 67, Saskatoon, Saskatchewan, S7K 3K1. E-mail: grainmag@sasktel.net Web site: www.grainmagazine.ca

The Malahat Review is a quarterly journal of contemporary poetry and fiction by both new and celebrated writers. Summer issues feature the winners of *Malahat*'s Novella and Long Poem Prizes, held in alternate years; all issues feature covers by noted Canadian visual artists and include reviews of Canadian books. Editor: Marlene Cookshaw. Assistant Editor: Lucy Bashford. Submissions and correspondence: *The Malahat Review*, University of Victoria, P.O. Box 1700, Station CSC, Victoria, British Columbia, V8W 2Y2. Web site: web.uvic.ca/malahat

The New Quarterly publishes fiction, poetry, interviews, and essays on writing. A two-time winner of the gold medal for fiction at the National Magazine Awards, with silver medals for fiction, poetry, and the essay, the magazine prides itself on its independent take on the Canadian literary scene. Recent achievements include the spectacular double issue "Wild Writers We Have Known," in which twenty-two writers who have worked extensively in the short story genre talked about what makes it work – and how. Editor: Kim Jernigan. Submissions and correspondence: *The New Quarterly*, c/o St. Jerome's University, 200 University Avenue West, Waterloo, Ontario, N2L 3G3. E-mail: newquart@watarts.uwaterloo.ca Web site: newquarterly.uwaterloo.ca

Queen's Quarterly, founded in 1893, is the oldest intellectual journal in Canada. It publishes articles on a variety of subjects and consequently fiction occupies relatively little space. There are one or two stories in each issue. However, because of its lively format and eclectic mix of subject matter, *Queen's Quarterly* attracts readers with widely diverse interests. This exposure is an advantage many of our fiction writers appreciate. Submissions are welcome from both new and established writers.

Fiction Editor: Joan Harcourt. Submissions and correspondence: *Queen's Quarterly*, Queen's University, 144 Barrie Street, Kingston, Ontario, K7L 3N6. Web site: info.queensu.ca/quarterly

This Magazine is one of Canada's longest-publishing magazines of politics, culture, and the arts. Over the years, *This Magazine* has introduced the early work of some of Canada's most notable writers, poets, and critics, including Margaret Atwood, Naomi Klein, Dennis Lee, Lillian Allen, Tomson Highway, Evelyn Lau, Dionne Brand, Michael Ondaatje, Mark Kingwell, Lynn Crosbie, Lynn Coady, and Jason Sherman. *This Magazine* publishes new fiction in every issue, and poetry three times a year, as well as an annual literary supplement in the September/October issue. The magazine does not accept unsolicited submissions of fiction, poetry, or drama, but new writers are encouraged to enter the magazine's annual contest, The Great Canadian Literary Hunt. Editor: Julie Crysler. Submissions and correspondence: *This Magazine*, 401 Richmond St. W., #396, Toronto, Ontario, M5V 3A8. Web site: www.thismag.org

Submissions were also received from the following journals:

Algonquin Roundtable Review
(Nepean, Ont.)

The Antigonish Review
(Antigonish, N.S.)

The Capilano Review
(North Vancouver, B.C.)

filling Station
(Calgary, Alta.)

Green's Magazine
(Regina, Sask.)

Matrix
(Montreal, Que.)

The New Orphic Review
(Nelson, B.C.)

On Spec Magazine
(Edmonton, Alta.)

Pagitica in Toronto
(Toronto, Ont.)

Parchment
(Toronto, Ont.)

Pottersfield Portfolio
(Sydney, N.S.)

Prairie Fire
(Winnipeg, Man.)

Prairie Journal
(Calgary, Alta.)

PRISM international
(Vancouver, B.C.)

Queen Street Quarterly
(Toronto, Ont.)

Storyteller
(Ottawa, Ont.)

Taddle Creek
(Toronto, Ont.)

TickleAce
(St. John's, Nfld.)

The Journey Prize Anthology
List of Previous Contributing Authors

* Winners of the $10,000 Journey Prize
** Co-winners of the $10,000 Journey Prize

I

1989

SELECTED WITH ALISTAIR MACLEOD

Ven Begamudré, "Word Games"
David Bergen, "Where You're From"
Lois Braun, "The Pumpkin-Eaters"
Constance Buchanan, "Man with Flying Genitals"
Ann Copeland, "Obedience"
Marion Douglas, "Flags"
Frances Itani, "An Evening in the Café"
Diane Keating, "The Crying Out"
Thomas King, "One Good Story, That One"
Holley Rubinsky, "Rapid Transits"*
Jean Rysstad, "Winter Baby"
Kevin Van Tighem, "Whoopers"
M.G. Vassanji, "In the Quiet of a Sunday Afternoon"
Bronwen Wallace, "Chicken 'N' Ribs"
Armin Wiebe, "Mouse Lake"
Budge Wilson, "Waiting"

2

1990

SELECTED WITH LEON ROOKE; GUY VANDERHAEGHE

André Alexis, "Despair: Five Stories of Ottawa"
Glen Allen, "The Hua Guofeng Memorial Warehouse"
Marusia Bociurkiw, "Mama, Donya"
Virgil Burnett, "Billfrith the Dreamer"
Margaret Dyment, "Sacred Trust"
Cynthia Flood, "My Father Took a Cake to France"*

Douglas Glover, "Story Carved in Stone"
Terry Griggs, "Man with the Axe"
Rick Hillis, "Limbo River"
Thomas King, "The Dog I Wish I Had, I Would Call It Helen"
K.D. Miller, "Sunrise Till Dark"
Jennifer Mitton, "Let Them Say"
Lawrence O'Toole, "Goin' to Town with Katie Ann"
Kenneth Radu, "A Change of Heart"
Jenifer Sutherland, "Table Talk"
Wayne Tefs, "Red Rock and After"

3
1991
SELECTED WITH JANE URQUHART

Donald Aker, "The Invitation"
Anton Baer, "Yukon"
Allan Barr, "A Visit from Lloyd"
David Bergen, "The Fall"
Rai Berzins, "Common Sense"
Diana Hartog, "Theories of Grief"
Diane Keating, "The Salem Letters"
Yann Martel, "The Facts Behind the Helsinki Roccamatios"*
Jennifer Mitton, "Polaroid"
Sheldon Oberman, "This Business with Elijah"
Lynn Podgurny, "Till Tomorrow, Maple Leaf Mills"
James Riseborough, "She Is Not His Mother"
Patricia Stone, "Living on the Lake"

4
1992
SELECTED WITH SANDRA BIRDSELL

David Bergen, "The Bottom of the Glass"
Maria A. Billion, "No Miracles Sweet Jesus"
Judith Cowan, "By the Big River"
Steven Heighton, "A Man Away from Home Has No Neighbours"
Steven Heighton, "How Beautiful upon the Mountains"
L. Rex Kay, "Travelling"

Rozena Maart, "No Rosa, No District Six"*
Guy Malet De Carteret, "Rainy Day"
Carmelita McGrath, "Silence"
Michael Mirolla, "A Theory of Discontinuous Existence"
Diane Juttner Perreault, "Bella's Story"
Eden Robinson, "Traplines"

5
1993
SELECTED WITH GUY VANDERHAEGHE

Caroline Adderson, "Oil and Dread"
David Bergen, "La Rue Prevette"
Marina Endicott, "With the Band"
Dayv James-French, "Cervine"
Michael Kenyon, "Durable Tumblers"
K.D. Miller, "A Litany in Time of Plague"
Robert Mullen, "Flotsam"
Gayla Reid, "Sister Doyle's Men"*
Oakland Ross, "Bang-bang"
Robert Sherrin, "Technical Battle for Trial Machine"
Carol Windley, "The Etruscans"

6
1994
SELECTED WITH DOUGLAS GLOVER;
JUDITH CHANT (CHAPTERS)

Anne Carson, "Water Margins: An Essay on Swimming by
    My Brother"
Richard Cumyn, "The Sound He Made"
Genni Gunn, "Versions"
Melissa Hardy, "Long Man the River"*
Robert Mullen, "Anomie"
Vivian Payne, "Free Falls"
Jim Reil, "Dry"
Robyn Sarah, "Accept My Story"
Joan Skogan, "Landfall"
Dorothy Speak, "Relatives in Florida"
Alison Wearing, "Notes from Under Water"

7

1995

SELECTED WITH M. G. VASSANJI;

RICHARD BACHMANN (A DIFFERENT DRUMMER BOOKS)

Michelle Alfano, "Opera"

Mary Borsky, "Maps of the Known World"

Gabriella Goliger, "Song of Ascent"

Elizabeth Hay, "Hand Games"

Shaena Lambert, "The Falling Woman"

Elise Levine, "Boy"

Roger Burford Mason, "The Rat-Catcher's Kiss"

Antanas Sileika, "Going Native"

Kathryn Woodward, "Of Marranos and Gilded Angels"*

8

1996

SELECTED WITH OLIVE SENIOR;

BEN McNALLY (NICHOLAS HOARE LTD.)

Rick Bowers, "Dental Bytes"

David Elias, "How I Crossed Over"

Elyse Gasco, "Can You Wave Bye Bye, Baby?"*

Danuta Gleed, "Bones"

Elizabeth Hay, "The Friend"

Linda Holeman, "Turning the Worm"

Elaine Littman, "The Winner's Circle"

Murray Logan, "Steam"

Rick Maddocks, "Lessons from the Sputnik Diner"

K.D. Miller, "Egypt Land"

Gregor Robinson, "Monster Gaps"

Alma Subasic, "Dust"

9

1997

SELECTED WITH NINO RICCI;

NICHOLAS PASHLEY (UNIVERSITY OF TORONTO BOOKSTORE)

Brian Bartlett, "Thomas, Naked"

Dennis Bock, "Olympia"

Kristen den Hartog, "Wave"

Gabriella Goliger, "Maladies of the Inner Ear" **
Terry Griggs, "Momma Had a Baby"
Mark Anthony Jarman, "Righteous Speedboat"
Judith Kalman, "Not for Me a Crown of Thorns"
Andrew Mullins, "The World of Science"
Sasenarine Persaud, "Canada Geese and Apple Chatney"
Anne Simpson, "Dreaming Snow" **
Sarah Withrow, "Ollie"
Terence Young, "The Berlin Wall"

10
1998
SELECTED BY PETER BUITENHUIS; HOLLEY RUBINSKY;
CELIA DUTHIE (DUTHIE BOOKS LTD.)

John Brooke, "The Finer Points of Apples" *
Ian Colford, "The Reason for the Dream"
Libby Creelman, "Cruelty"
Michael Crummey, "Serendipity"
Stephen Guppy, "Downwind"
Jane Eaton Hamilton, "Graduation"
Elise Levine, "You Are You Because Your Little Dog Loves You"
Jean McNeil, "Bethlehem"
Liz Moore, "Eight-Day Clock"
Edward O'Connor, "The Beatrice of Victoria College"
Tim Rogers, "Scars and Other Presents"
Denise Ryan, "Marginals, Vivisections, and Dreams"
Madeleine Thien, "Simple Recipes"
Cheryl Tibbetts, "Flowers of Africville"

11
1999
SELECTED BY LESLEY CHOYCE; SHELDON CURRIE;
MARY-JO ANDERSON (FROG HOLLOW BOOKS)

Mike Barnes, "In Florida"
Libby Creelman, "Sunken Island"
Mike Finigan, "Passion Sunday"
Jane Eaton Hamilton, "Territory"

Mark Anthony Jarman, "Travels into Several Remote Nations of
the World"

Barbara Lambert, "Where the Bodies Are Kept"

Linda Little, "The Still"

Larry Lynch, "The Sitter"

Sandra Sabatini, "The One With the News"

Sharon Steams, "Brothers"

Mary Walters, "Show Jumping"

Alissa York, "The Back of the Bear's Mouth" *

12
2000
SELECTED BY CATHERINE BUSH; HAL NIEDZVIECKI;
MARC GLASSMAN (PAGES BOOKS AND MAGAZINES)

Andrew Gray, "The Heart of the Land"

Lee Henderson, "Sheep Dub"

Jessica Johnson, "We Move Slowly"

John Lavery, "The Premier's New Pyjamas"

J.A. McCormack, "Hearsay"

Nancy Richler, "Your Mouth Is Lovely"

Andrew Smith, "Sightseeing"

Karen Solie, "Onion Calendar"

Timothy Taylor, "Doves of Townsend" *

Timothy Taylor, "Pope's Own"

Timothy Taylor, "Silent Cruise"

R.M. Vaughan, "Swan Street"

13
2001
SELECTED BY ELYSE GASCO; MICHAEL HELM;
MICHAEL NICHOLSON (INDIGO BOOKS & MUSIC INC.)

Kevin Armstrong, "The Cane Field" *

Mike Barnes, "Karaoke Mon Amour"

Heather Birrell, "Machaya"

Heather Birrell, "The Present Perfect"

Craig Boyko, "The Gun"

Vivette J. Kady, "Anything That Wiggles"